WHEN KINGS RISE
VI CARTER

CARTER BOOKS

CONTENTS

BLURB

MY RIVALS ARE DONS; I am a King.

Three brides have been chosen for my pleasure and displeasure. One of them will become a King's consort, and the others will be discarded.

Until my decision is made, I get to feast on them all.

They are mine.

After the demise of my uncle, the O'Sullivan family has yet to choose the new Don. With two brothers and a vengeful, unhinged cousin also vying for the position, tension is rising in an already dangerous business.

Especially since no one knows that I'm responsible for my uncle's disappearance.

Enter the Hands of Kings, a global cult with the ability to replace CEOs, Presidents, and Popes. And their leader, Victor, has his eye on me.

Few men were made to be Kings and Victor has plans for me, plans that do not require my approval.

But an unseen enemy is hiding, and they know my secrets. They are manipulating the people around me with the intention of taking my crown.

A King is not so easily dethroned, though, especially when threats are made toward me and mine.

No one shall have my brides.

When Kings Rise is a dark mafia romance intensified by the presence of a cult. It has mature themes, mature language, and very mature steam.

CHAPTER ONE

DIARMUID

Hands of the Kings Edict One

> *The Hand of Kings is not a political movement, rebellion, or cult. It is a natural order of life. Just as the moon and sun command the heavens, the Kings command the Earth.*

THERE IS ALWAYS A sense of peace in chaos.

Quiet chaos, that's what I walk into in the grand ballroom on the top floor of the mansion. A part of me wished this could be done in my home, but that would be unheard of. The showing of the brides was always at the Hand of the Kings' mansion.

The long red velvet curtains have been drawn. The gold weights that keep the curtains in place, still shifting along the oak flooring inside their lining, tell me they have only recently been pulled to plunge the room into a romantic darkness.

Nonsense really.

The candles along the walls have been lit—hundreds of them—more nonsense, but this is what the arriving brides are accustomed to— or so I've heard. A room shimmering in romance, but their shaking figures scream anything but that.

That is their way, their duty. I run my thumb along my lip as I think about our traditions. Every King is given three candidates who must show obedience at all times. How many kings are there? That I'm not sure of.

But right now, my three brides are obedient.

All their gazes are downcast, which is what is expected. They will only look at me when I request it. I take my time glancing at the portraits of all the past leaders that hang along the walls. Their eyes follow my every move. They don't intimidate me; they are the past, and I am the future.

The final three pictures, however, do give me pause. The first is Andrew O'Sullivan, who was the head of the family until his recent disappearance. A twinge of a smile dances along my lips, but I suppress it as I stop in front of the final two paintings. One is of Richard O'Sullivan, my father, whom everyone assumed would one day take over.

I chuckle. *"You know what they say about assuming things."* Beside him is my mother, Elise O'Sullivan.

I stare at her face, the steel gray eyes that I inherited from her. All else I received from her was hate. Hate for how she allowed men to take me, shape me, and damage me. She never protected me. No one did. But I would have expected some form of protection from her as my mother.

I place my hands behind my back and walk past the row of servants. Seven, to be exact. Once I reach the final one, the first turns, and the rest fall into line, leaving the room. Leaving me alone with my prizes. They are not just servants; each is chosen carefully and skilled in a variety of ways to take a life. Working in the mansion of the "Hands of the Kings" requires knowledge of how to kill—wolves in sheep's clothing.

I continue my walk to the waiting brides.

One of them I will have to marry, but until that moment, I get to play, and like my brothers would admit, I don't play nicely. I keep walking the distance until I'm in front of the three naked ladies. The one in the center has her hands folded across her private area. Like she has any right to shield herself from me. These women have been bred for this, so she should know better.

"Place your hands at your sides." Her response is instant, and her dusky Mediterranean skin flows along her graceful arms that hang loosely, fingertips grazing her thighs. "It's not a good sign when you have to be corrected already." I let out a bored sigh, and she flicks a glance up at me before focusing on the floor at her bare feet. She may be the troublesome one.

The troublemaker.

I hide a grin.

"Troublemaker, what is your name?" She glances up.

"Selene." Her voice is soft. Her eyes aren't the only part of her that is hostile. The shape of her shoulders and how they slouch forward like she can shield herself from my gaze isn't lost on me.

"I think I prefer Troublemaker," I say.

She holds my gaze for a beat more before diverting her attention to her toes. I follow her line of vision, and her toes tense along the hard oak flooring. This room is accustomed to polished shoes and dancing heels, not bare feet. She shivers, and I wonder if it is the cold or fear. Long dark brown hair is neatly arranged on top of her head. Pinned back almost severely. Nothing can shield her face from me.

Fires have been lit in the room, all three send out a soft wave of heat. One reaches the side of my face and I almost want to bat it away. I prefer no fires in my own private rooms. But this isn't my home, so I don't have a say.

I move on to the next girl. She reminds me of a statue with how she holds herself so still. Her fingers seem to move involuntarily along her side. Her nerves are getting the best of her. I pass her and stop at the final bride.

She looks at me directly. "What is your full name?" I ask.

"Amira Reardon." She has soft brown eyes and an oval, innocent-looking face. She won't be very innocent when I'm finished with her. Her complexion is pale, yet under the glow of the light, it appears slightly tanned. Once she says her name, she averts her gaze, but not before I catch something dark and intelligent hiding behind her eyes.

My darkness recognizes something inside her. Damage.

I go back two steps and stand in front of the woman who is first. She hasn't moved a muscle. She reminds me of a beautiful statue. All angles and posture. She has an athletic structure. Her long blonde hair hangs loosely around her shoulders. "Look at me," I say.

She keeps her gaze downcast, but she squeezes her thighs together. I reach in and touch her chin, tilting her face toward me until I'm looking into brown eyes.

"You must be Niamh Connolly. Ms. Connolly, my name is Diarmuid O'Sullivan, and it would be wise to listen to me when I give you a command."

I release her chin and walk in front of the three of them, taking in their beautiful bodies and faces. These are the brides chosen for me by Victor Madigan and Wolf O'Sullivan. I will get to know all of them, and in the end, I will only choose one. They were selected very carefully. I don't particularly like the idea of Victor or Wolf selecting anything for me. I can't stand either of them. But it's our hierarchy, and Victor is the head of the Hand of Kings, so he isn't someone I can ever question. Even if I was dissatisfied with his choice.

I'm not. All three are stunning, perfect...hopefully, they are obedient, too.

I return to the troublemaker, Selene. "Look at me," I command. She does, but there is no longer a fire in her gaze. She has tucked that away. She learns quickly. Now, she wears a blank look on her face, like she is facing her execution. I take in her beauty, allowing myself as much time as I wish to study her body before bringing my attention back to her hair.

"Let your hair down."

There is a flash of fear, but Selene raises her hands and removes each pin. One pings along the oak flooring. The noise has Amira glancing in our direction. When I catch her eye, she quickly looks away.

Selene holds all the pins in her hands, and I watch her beauty transform and grow as silky, wavy brown hair cascades down her back.

"I bet that feels better?" I ask.

She gives a quick nod of her head, but her pulse flickers wildly along her neck.

I'm ready to move on but the fire in her gaze grows again. I don't like fire. I want to extinguish it. Fire is uncontrollable, and to survive in our world you need control. My bride will need control. This lesson will anger Selene, I'm sure, but in time will teach her a lesson.

"Touch yourself," I command.

She uses the hand that is fisted with pins and slides her knuckles along her private area. "Use your other hand," I order.

She swallows and closes her eyes.

"Keep looking at me while you touch yourself, Selene."

Her eyelids flutter open, and her free hand runs along her mound. My cock grows instantly. I close the distance between us and grip her hand. With my other one, I grab her thigh, and she spreads her legs, giving both our hands access. I hold only one of her fingers and push it inside her opening. She inhales sharply. I let the tip of my finger follow hers, and the moisture that greets me makes me want to take more. To explore the warmth that tightens around my finger. I pull out and sink back in while looking into her eyes. Her cheeks are tinged with pink, but her gaze is steady. Control. That's exactly what I want to see. I withdraw. She doesn't. She's smart.

"Keep going, Selene," I order, and she takes her finger out before pushing it back in.

"Amira," I say. Her childlike features remind me of a porcelain doll. She doesn't belong here, maybe on a shelf in a child's room. A part of me can't wait to corrupt her, yet that darkness that I saw earlier is there and makes me curious about her. "Watch Selene." Amira does, and I stop in front of Niamh.

"Do you want to join Selene?" I ask.

I like watching her brown eyes swirl with fear. "Do… I have to?" She has a stammer; it's a flaw, but I like flaws.

I run my thumb along my lip. "You answered a question with a question," I bite back.

She moves instantly, and I take in her toned oval ass. She must be athletic. I wonder what sports she favors. She moves quickly to Selene but pauses in front of her. Selene is making great work of stimulating herself. If I were to guess, I'd say she was enjoying it.

Niamh peeks at me before she reaches out with a shaky hand and touches Selene's breast. She squeezes it, showing she has never touched a breast before.

I walk back to them, and they both pause. My gaze darkens, and they continue the show for me.

I grip Selene's free breasts at the base and drag my hand upwards, tightening until I reach the nipple and squeeze. Selene hisses with pleasure.

"Just like that, Niamh."

Niamh copies me, and I can already tell she is going to be a very good student. I reach down and cover Selene's hand. Pulling her finger out of her opening, they are soaking, and I push her wet finger against her swollen bud. I keep my hand over hers as I circle her sensitive area while Niamh repeats the action on Selene's breasts.

I look at Amira, who's watching. Her mouth forms a small *oh*. She catches me looking at her, and it's clear in her gaze that she wants to be part of this, but for that reason, I don't invite her. I don't stop until Selene shudders on her hand and her orgasm ceases.

I step back and give a short clap.

"Very well done, Selene; maybe you aren't a trouble-maker after all." My cock bulges against my trousers.

Maybe Amira could have her first lesson in pleasing me. As I take a step toward her, my phone rings. I scoop it out of my pocket and turn my back on my three brides.

It's Wolf. I assume he's ringing to see what I think of his selection.

"I can't fucking believe it." That's Wolf's opening line.

I step toward the red velvet curtains.

"I don't know who would do this." He sounds upset. Almost distraught.

I don't care. I like hearing him this distraught.

"They found my father, Diarmuid. He's dead."

I knew this moment would arrive. "Are you sure?" I ask.

"What?"

"Are you sure he's dead? Did you see his body?" I ask.

"Yes, he was pulled out of a shallow grave. Yes, he's very fucking dead," Wolf snaps.

I turn to my three brides, who are back in formation. Selene looks flushed. Perfect in the light.

I hadn't time to dig any deeper, but a shallow grave is all that Andrew O'Sullivan deserved.

CHAPTER TWO

AMIRA

A WAVE RISES HARD and fast, and I clench my fists so I don't strike my own face like I want to. I can't react, not with one of my guards' thighs pressed firmly against mine.

My vision wavers, and I sneer at how weak I am. I failed today.

"Don't you always." A voice whispers in my mind.

I straighten my spine, my mind ruminating on the moment that Diarmuid had given all his attention to the other two girls and not me.

I want a mirror to check my face. I'm pretty—I know that—so what didn't he like? A lot of people see me as angelic and innocent, and I play that part so well. Maybe not well enough this time. Diarmuid had looked at me with a tilt of his head like he had seen through the porcelain skin and bright brown eyes to the real me.

I divert my gaze to my lap and flex my fingers. Next time, I need to do better.

After seeing Diarmuid O'Sullivan, I know with every fiber of my being that I want to be his. I will win my place as his bride.

The darkness around the vehicle sinks deeper inside, casting too many shadows. I'm tempted to reach up and flick on the small overhead light, but I remain still. I know if I make a move, I will lose the last shred of my control.

My heart thumps as we travel down the winding road that opens a bit wider. Trees bend toward the vehicle, their long, bare branches like claws reaching out to me.

The vehicle slows, taking a left turn, past wrought iron gates that once shined with a polished black varnish, but now, the peeling paint makes a line across the driveway that gets crushed under the wheels of the heavy vehicle as we pass.

I don't want to go home. I smash my eyelids tighter and conjure the image of Diarmuid O'Sullivan. My heart rate slows, and a sense of peace flows across my chest. The cogs of my heart loosen, and a smile plays on my lips.

He's so handsome, like a prince from a fairytale who has come to take me away.

Thump, thump thump. My heart threatens to start racing again, and I will it to settle. I only have seconds before we reach my home, and I want them to be quiet seconds.

Diarmuid's gray eyes are like the marble tops of my kitchen counters: soft, pretty, and soothing. My core tightens as I remember his large frame entering the room. He would be powerful on top of me. His shoulders wide and his arms strong. The vehicle comes to a stop, shattering my moment, and I open my eyes.

I glance up at my home. The estate house shrouded in darkness is beautiful. A light shines from the second floor. It's my welcome home. The light of my sanctuary, my bedroom, that I left on. It's the only welcome I will receive.

The pressure against my thigh is relieved as my guard gets out. The driver opens my door, and I step out into a soft but sharp breeze. I roll my shoulders and imagine armor materializing on my shoulders and spreading across my chest.

The front door is opened for me, and I turn to see the guard sink into the darkness as he takes his station beside the front door. The driver doesn't enter but returns to take the car to the garage.

I close the door, and the sound is loud. I turn to the darkened hall. I must win Diarmuid's heart; I must be his bride. The words repeat in my mind with each step I take into our estate home. It once was beautifully maintained, but it crumbled when my father fell apart. He left our family in ruins, and I intend to turn this all around for us.

I nod to myself; I will fix what he destroyed.

My foot touches the first step of the staircase that leads to my room, but I pause and listen to the low hum of the house. Pipes gurgle somewhere deep in the mansion. A breeze touches my back, and I turn to the main drawing room. Inside, it's dark, but I find the source of the breeze. One of the windows has been left ajar.

I push the heavy gold drapes aside, and a scattering of dust flutters down on top of me, making me cough. I ignore the assault on my lungs , grab the handle of the window, and yank it toward me. It doesn't budge but creaks in resistance. A chair is in my way, and I push it aside to get closer. Using both hands, I pull, and the window slams shut.

I push the handle down and lock the window. Another cough erupts as I step back from the window that overlooks the garden. Weeds merge with once-blossoming flower beds, and the hedge line coexists with trees and hangs down onto the overgrown lawn. I want to pull the drapes so I don't have to look at the offending state of the grounds, but I'm sure the dust would suffocate me. I turn to the rows of bookshelves. They, too, have their very own coating of dust. The books that line the shelves are not for reading pleasure but for decoration. My father bought them for their visual appeal, not the words that are printed between the hardbacks.

I crave the privacy of my room, away from the dust and musty smell of our home.

I pause in the hallway as my stomach rumbles. I haven't eaten. The nerves earlier today didn't allow me to even have a sip of water.

The kitchen has a lamp on the counter that spreads a small amount of light. The overhead chandelier is in darkness, its bulbs long blown, and no one to replace them.

I open the fridge and find some fresh ham I had bought two days ago. If I hadn't ventured into our local village, we would starve. I close the fridge door and pause. There is something different. It's not something I can see but smell first. Vodka has such a distinctive smell to me, and I scan the darkened corners and stop when my mother appears from the other side of the kitchen.

My mother stares at me, and my fingers tighten around the ham.

She snorts before she speaks. "Eating again, I see?"

The glass hangs loosely from her fingers as she walks toward me with a snarl plastered on her face. "A fat bride isn't really a good look."

I'm tempted to look down at my frame. I always make sure I stay close to 1000 calories a day to remain slim.

"I haven't eaten today." My voice is so frail, and I hate it.

"You look like you eat plenty to me. Put the ham back."

I don't want to fight, and I do as she says. I'm ready to walk away as she laughs. It's cruel, slurred, and intended to hurt.

It finds its mark, and my stomach clenches.

"I never thought my own daughter would be a whore."

I think of how Diarmuid favored the other girls, how he never touched me. I wish he had. I wish he had made me feel something beyond what I always feel—Insignificant.

"Isn't that what you raised me to be, Mother?" My bold words give me a moment of satisfaction. I didn't choose to be a bride; my parents handed me over on a platter. Just like they had my brothers. The thought of my brothers sends another wave of grief through me. Grief that I have never been allowed to deal with. My father is mafia, my brothers were recruited into the Hands of the Kings, and being part of the organization took my brothers' lives. It's our world. Now, it might take mine.

She marches to me, and my bravery dies quickly, it becomes a pool around my ankles on the grimy kitchen floor.

"I gave you everything. The best parts of me." She runs a hand through her thinning hair. She once was a woman men stopped to look at for her beauty; now they look for a different reason. They look down on us, the family who fell from grace by the hand of a king.

"When you have a daughter, they say she takes your beauty away, and didn't you do that to me?" She grips my face and tightens her fingers painfully along my jaw. "You don't deserve my beauty."

I pull my face away from her. "Goodnight, Mother." I've heard this since I was a child. How I stole her beauty and grace. My brothers, of course, didn't—only me. I took everything from her as I grew in her womb. When my brothers died, her grief manifested into a deeper hate for me, along with her indulgence of alcohol.

"All of a sudden, you think you can treat me like this." Her anger grows. "You think because you are a whore to the O'Sullivans, that you can just walk away from me."

I stand my ground as she rants, and when her glass flies from her fingers and smashes against the counter, I flinch.

"Disgusting." She's irate, and I want to leave but try to make myself small so I don't anger her further. My shoulders hunch closer to my chest, but I'm never going to be small enough.

My silence has her anger swelling; her hand strikes my face once, twice before she falls into a heap at my feet, sobbing. My face burns, and I step around her.

"Don't walk away from me," she calls, but the violence has left her words, and sobs rack her frame. I don't stop walking. I make it to the stairs when I hear cabinet doors banging. She's looking for more vodka. She hides bottles throughout the house but forgets where she left them.

I've found them in most corners of the house and enjoy pouring each bottle down the toilet. I often hear her frantically searching the house and smashing things in her search for her poison.

My bedroom is well—lit, and the bed neatly made. I close the door behind me and turn the lock—not that she would ever come into my room, but I won't ever allow her to spoil this space for me.

I walk to the window and draw the curtains before entering my small ensuite. Taking a fresh face cloth from the top stack, I turn on the hot water, but only cold water pours out. I soak the cloth before rinsing out as much moisture as possible.

Taking a seat at my vanity that's tidy and polished, I curse her as the red welt on my face burns. My stomach rumbles but I won't venture back downstairs. I'll have to wait until morning.

I meet my gaze in the mirror. "Let's fix you up." I smile at my reflection and dab my cloth against my face. The burn intensifies, and I remove it.

A child's nursery tune comes to mind, and I hum as I clean my face. When I can't do anymore, I open my jar of night cream and rub it carefully on the welt as I continue to hum. When the cream dries, I paint on my makeup; using a soft brush, I apply blusher across the wound before blending in the makeup. Placing a small dab of gray eyeshadow on my lids, I stare at my reflection as I apply a coat of red lipstick. I don't look so innocent now. I look fierce. I smile at myself. This is the color I will wear the next time I meet Diarmuid. He needs to see me, and these bold colors will make him take notice.

I lean across the vanity and kiss my reflection. I giggle at my lipstick mark on the glass. Using the cloth, I wipe the lipstick away.

He will notice me next time.

"Yes, he will," I say to my reflection.

CHAPTER THREE

DIARMUID

Hands of the Kings Edict Two

> *Any sin can be forgiven except for the sin of abandonment. The wrongdoer will feel the abandonment of the order for three generations.*

I TURN off THE engine and climb out of my car. It's low to the ground and when I rise to my full height, I can easily see all around me. The gardens here sprawl further than my eye can see. They are manicured yet hold a wildness to them that I know is intentional. It's a sham. My tolerance for fakeness is low.

I laugh at the thought, considering my life is one huge charade rolled in a thick carpet of fakeness. I glare at the valet, who waits for the keys to my car. I place the keys in his hand, and he folds his fingers around them. No fear shines in his gaze. It really shouldn't. No person here is what they seem. I know the valets can kill with their bare hands. Just like the other servants, they're trained killers. Everyone who works for the Kings is, but respect shines in his gaze. He knows who I am; he knows my capabilities. As the Hand of the King's assassin, I outrank him.

The Tudor—style structure before me was built to display wealth, and it didn't disappoint. I like luxury, but I don't like being at the Hand of the Kings' headquarters; this is my second time this week.

The purr of my engine has me looking back at my car as it disappears out of sight. The large driveaway has a wide arc that sweeps into the trees. This property is also designed to hide its guests from prying eyes, not that anyone would get onto this property without approval. It's more protected than the Vatican.

I would imagine the pope has a say here, too. I know that Victor controls the Kings below him, but I don't think he acts alone. That information was never given to any of the O'Sullivan's, or Kings, for that matter. We are on a need-to-know basis as far as who the Hands of Kings really are and how far their reach truly goes. I don't think it's just Ireland that they control; I always get a sense that it's a wider web that's cast across the world.

Edward, the doorman, offers to take my coat, and I hand it over with a raised eyebrow. He grins and tilts his head. He's a poison expert who has assassinated many important guests by hiding "treats" in their coats. Sometimes, the poison is on the coat and sinks into the skin; other times, it's a surprise in their pockets. I know I haven't anything to fear, so we jest.

I watch as the maid takes my coat from Edward and places it in a closet that's large enough to be a dining hall, but is lined with mostly empty rods for guests' coats, bags, and other belongings. The maid, who is also Edward's apprentice, disappears from view. She is skilled at turning her wrist and allowing something deadly to fall from her sleeve into your drink. A handy trick.

I walk through the foyer of the house, knowing there are four sets of eyes watching me at all times from the watchtower where the cameras are located. I'd been there as a child and had to map out this entire property with its hidden hallways and secret tunnels. It's how I get around easily if my skill is required, but mostly, I'm sent out into the world to take down anyone the House of the Kings deems an enemy. That's how I know their hold on the world is wider than just the Irish landscape. I've been sent almost everywhere in the world to take down their enemies.

I pause and glance up at the winding staircase that leads to the room where I had my first glimpse of my brides. Excitement curls in my stomach. They were all delicious, and they did as commanded so well. They were well-picked and clearly informed that their obedience was expected, no matter what I asked. The first meeting was a test, and one they all passed.

Usually, meetings are held in the grand dining room, where drinks and a meal are served. But not today. We are being ushered to the private study. As I step across the threshold, I brace myself for what is to come from this meeting.

It is late September. If the old man had ordered a fire lit, it would be stifling here. If a disagreement were to take place, someone in that room could end up with his face smashed against the grate.

I glance at the fireplace and am relieved to see the fire is out. The study is large considering there are a few couches, but not enough for the people attending the meeting.

A chair is vacant, and Edward's apprentice offers it to me in deference to my position. A part of me wants to sit to show my power, but I decline with a wave of my hand.

Standing is safer in a room filled with such deadly people. I won't make myself vulnerable. It's one of the lessons that is ingrained in me.

The crowd consists of the most powerful members of the Hands of Kings, excluding my brothers, who aren't here. I do, however, see my cousin Wolf across the room. Wolf catches my eye and nods toward me. I nod back and take a drink offered by another maid. I raise the glass in a toast to my cousin and bring it to my lips, but I don't drink from it. Wolf notices, as he has been watching me carefully, and gives me a wicked grin that I ignore.

The murmuring stops when a far door, a door not used by guests, opens. I brace myself, expecting to see the one person who can strike fear in me, but someone else steps out.

It's Michael Reardon, a page for the Hands of Kings.

"Isn't this a bit above your pay grade?" Wolf sounds offended as he turns to Michael. No one else speaks, and Michael's face reddens.

This gives Wolf more glee as he continues. "You have a lot of balls to use the crisis room when you are barely a member."

Michael can't respond. It's forbidden. A page is the lowest rank in the cult. Wolf is a Duke, son of the recently deceased King. It is an insult for a page to speak to a Duke.

Michael dips his head in a plea for forgiveness before he speaks. "I do apologize, Duke. The Hand himself would have come, but the situation is uncertain in the group."

Michael speaks out of turn, in my opinion. He should never make it sound like the Hand of the King is hiding. But everyone is as curious as I am as to what has made our leader hide.

"Uncertain?" Wolf barks before waving his hand across the waiting crowd. "Do enlighten us, Page," he sneers.

Michael looks ready to bolt from the room and glances back at the door he came from. It seems as if it's a reminder of the task he was given, so he addresses the room. "As you all know, almost a year ago, Andrew O'Sullivan disappeared," Michael speaks to the rest of the room and doesn't direct his attention to Wolf, who is fit to kill the page for just mentioning his father's name.

When Andrew disappeared, everyone thought he had either been killed or had gone into hiding as he controlled an illegal gambling ring, but nothing was ever confirmed.

"Three weeks ago, we got confirmation of his death," Michael says, and there is an audible intake of breath in the room.

I keep my hand relaxed around my drink, not reacting to the news. Three weeks ago? How had I not heard about this sooner?

"It's Andrew for certain?" One of the members asks in a small voice. They're trying to pretend like they care, but already, the scramble for power has begun. Who will align with whom, and what positions will become available with this turn of events?

"Yes, the gardai struggled to place his identity at first." For the first time, Michael looks at Wolf.

"Get on with it," Wolf barks, like we aren't discussing his father's brutal but well-deserved death.

"His head, fingertips, and toes were all removed. But luckily, one of our contacts in the gardai department reached out to the Kings. Richard O'Sullivan, Andrew's brother, provided a DNA sample. The body is that of Andrew Sullivan."

My father helped solve the crime and never informed me. I get many glances from the crowd, but when I continue to focus on Michael, they look away.

I was foolish. I should have buried the body deeper or done what I do best—make the body disappear. But anger and the need for revenge had made me sloppy.

"You can be assured that the Kings will be using all their resources to find the killer and find who set up the killer." Michael appears pleased with himself.

Set up the killer? I tense and try to relax my frame again.

Wolf places his drink down on the study desk, liquid sloshing across the rim of the glass.

"Wait, someone knows who the killer is?"

"A woman, currently unidentified, was found on top of Andrew's grave. She was placed perfectly above it. It's either a coincidence, or someone within the organization is telling the killer that they know who they are."

Once again, I control my body's reaction. This is all news to me. A guilty person would fail to make eye contact with the people around them. So, I look around the room at everyone. I'm assessing them, for a gleam in their eyes that might tell me they know my secret, but their greedy eyes shine as their own futures spin away in their minds. Some who have known Andrew a long time show rage, and some show fear. If someone in this room knows my secret, they are just as good at playing the game as I am.

"Thank you all for your time," Michael says, and the crowd starts to talk amongst one another. Michael meets my gaze and makes his way to me, dipping his head in respect at everyone he passes. I place my full glass on a nearby table.

"I have a message from Victor. He requests you to be at church on Sunday. And he wants you to bring one of your brides." His voice is low, the message for me and me alone, but the few around us are listening intently.

I nod in agreement, and Michael quickly departs. I don't linger in the room but leave. Edward has my coat ready when I arrive at the main door.

"I hope you had a good meeting?" He helps me slip into the coat.

I watch him, wondering if he knows. Someone placed a woman's body on top of the grave I dug. That is no coincidence. I'm getting a message; someone knows what I have done, and that's why they placed the body there, so it would be found along with Andrew's. I need to be careful and treat everyone as suspects. Once I find the person responsible, I will silence them. Making them completely disappear is my only option.

"It was eventful," I answer. "Tell the valet to bring my car."

"It's already waiting." Edward slips his hands behind his back. "I know how you like to leave as soon as possible."

He does, but that doesn't douse the suspicion that has risen in me. I nod and exit the mansion. Sure enough, my car is waiting. Once I'm inside, I take my phone out and look at the names of my three brides. I have to bring one of them to mass on Sunday.

I'm thinking of Selene, but remember she's a trouble-maker, and I don't need to draw attention to myself. Amira has a darkness that I will explore, but not now. So I choose Niamh.

CHAPTER FOUR

NIAMH

*B*LUE!

The color I adore, as it reminds me of the bottom of the swimming pool, a place where I can get lost in. There are no demands from the water; sounds are muffled, and at times, it silences my mind. My fingers tighten around the material, but the dress is too short for Sunday service. I fling it over my shoulder, and it joins the piles of dresses behind me.

The next item of clothing is a cream blouse, one my mother always hated as she declared it showed off far too much skin with its transparent material. This one I linger on longer, imagining her features pinching in complete disapproval.

I shake off the rebellious thought and throw the blouse onto the ground. A screech sounds, and I turn to see Scamps race out of the walk-in closet with the blouse covering his furry body.

I'm tempted to chase after the cat, but the sound of soft laughter has me staying put. "Come here, Scamps; what has she done to you?" My sister's soothing voice reaches my ears.

"Is she okay?" I call when I spot a silky blue scarf on the ground. I will take a piece of me to Sunday Service. I scoop it up off the floor and exit the walk-in closet with the only dress that falls below my knees. It will have to do. I nearly tumble across the piles of clothes that I have discarded in my search for appropriate clothing.

"She's fine," Ella speaks from my bed. She's lying on her stomach with her phone in hand. She doesn't look up at me as she grins and continues to scroll.

"You better not be posting that on social media," I warn.

Ella has turned Scamps into a cat star, or so she likes to think.

Ella still doesn't look up at me. "I won't," she lies.

I bet she snapped a picture of Scamps wearing my blouse.

I slip the dark blue dress over my head; it falls perfectly below my knee. I've already put on pantyhose, and I take the light silk scarf and tighten it around my neck. I have to return to the closet for my white gloves and hat. Once everything is on, I return to my bedroom.

"What do you think?" I ask.

For the first time, Ella looks up at me. Her eyes widen, and I feel like I've nailed it until she bursts out laughing. "What on God's green earth are you wearing?"

I glance down at my dress and brush imaginary wrinkles away. Dolores, our housemaid, would be appalled to think everything wasn't perfect; it always is, but my nerves are getting the best of me.

Ella rolls onto her back, her chuckles coming to a stop when she sits up, but she still wears a goofy smile. Her soft brown eyes and sandy blonde hair are identical to mine.

"Church clothes!" I hold my arms out as if to say, isn't it obvious?

"It's not the Christ child's birthday, is it? No one goes to church like that on a September Sunday."

I place my hands on my hips. "How would I know? We are not exactly church people. Besides, how would you know?"

Ella raises her phone, and I quickly try to grab the contraption before she takes a picture of me. She pulls it out of my reach, but I'm satisfied when she places it on my bed. "Every time I sleep over Riley's house, her mother insists on us attending Mass in order to save my poor soul. Just put on a nice sweater and brush your teeth, and everyone will be cool with you. Trust me."

I allow my hands to run across my dress one more time. Maybe this is too much. "Even if I am going with someone like Diarmuid O'Sullivan?" I hate how I stammer over his name. The memory of what I did with Selene turns my face red, and I dip my chin, the hat hopefully hiding my burning cheeks from my sister.

"I mean…maybe keep the dress? Definitely get rid of the gloves and hat. You look like Nan." Ella's voice has softened.

I pull off the hat and the gloves and sit down beside Ella on the bed. There is a comfortable silence between us. I imagine she's thinking about how one day she may be handed over to a strange man just like me. It's not the future I want for my sister. I wrap my arm around her shoulder and lean my head against hers. "What would I do without you?" She is the reason I am going through with this. I will not allow her to be handed over to a strange man. If I do this for our family's position, then she won't have to.

"Probably end up with a husband with no teeth, especially if you dress like that."

I release Ella as she chuckles again. The dress isn't that bad. "Oh my God, let it go," I warn her as I return to the mirror.

"Sorry, sis. I have a visual memory, and that was quite a visual."

I meet Ella's gaze in the mirror. She's no longer smiling; she has picked up her phone but hasn't turned it on. I spin, leaving my own worries to the side, and focus on Ella.

"How many hours today?"

Ella shrugs her shoulders before she speaks. "Four. I got lucky. My recital went well, and Mother is pleased. Sunday is supposed to be my one day off from ballet, but she still wants four hours in the basement."

Guilt churns heavily in my stomach. It should be me, is all I can think. "That sounds rough." I finally say. But I remind myself I can't save her from everything. So, the tradeoff isn't so bad. She must do dance instead of being handed over to the hands of the kings.

Ella sighs and looks at me sadly. "It could be worse."

She's sixteen; she should be having fun, playing on her phone, hanging out with friends like an ordinary teenager, but we aren't ordinary. I don't think we ever will be. Our mother demands perfection in the form of extracurricular activities that she craved during her youth. She lives her life through us. Ballet was her love, and I had to endure years of training, but now that I'm being married off, I was allowed to step away, but only at the expense of Ella picking up the exhausting training.

"When will he be here?" Ella changes the subject, reminding me how wise she is beyond her years.

I glance at the dainty gold watch that wraps my wrist, a gift from my father on my twenty-first birthday.

I exhale. "Soon. I need to get downstairs." I pick up a pair of small black kitten heels and slip my feet into them.

"Niamh?"

Ella's soft voice has me picking up my clutch and pausing before I leave the room. "Yeah?"
"I hope he is kind to you."

My throat tightens at her words. "I hope so too, kid." I leave the room before I start to cry. I won't break. I go down to the main floor and walk to the back of the house, where I can see through plate-glass windows. In the distance, the Irish Sea laps gently against the shores of Dublin. I close my eyes and think about the taste of the salt on my lips. The weight of the water against my body, the freedom the ocean offers me. Freedom that I can't find in this world.

The doorbell rings, startling me out of my meditation. I leave my favorite room and make my way gracefully to the front door. Years of being a ballerina and advanced swimmer have given my footing grace and poise that makes me look sure and calm. I am neither on the inside.

I take one final glance at my reflection in the hall mirror as the doorbell rings again. I'm not one to wear makeup, so I've kept it light, with a single coat of gloss across my lips and a thin application of mascara. With my hair swept up in a knot at the nape of my neck, I look composed and respectful. I open the door, expecting to see Diarmuid O'Sullivan's driver, but I'm taken aback to find the man himself on my doorstep. The night I met him, a driver had collected me from my home, so I expected the same today.

His gray eyes take me in from the tip of my toes all the way to the crown of my head. I hold still, remembering the level of respect we must show him. The obedience we must give. That part was drilled into my head by my parents. I hate it, but to keep Ella safe, I will do what is necessary. His Armani gray suit is almost the same color as his eyes. I don't want this marriage, but that doesn't stop me from admiring how handsome he is. I smile like I'm at the start of a show and compose all my nerves.

"Good evening, Mr. O'Sullivan." I don't stutter, and for that, I'm grateful.

"Miss Connelly." His voice is deep and sends shivers across my flesh. I grip my clutch and step out onto the porch; he turns his back on me as I close the door.

Diarmuid walks to his car and opens the passenger door for me; he's driving us himself. This will make us very close. I get into the passenger seat and thank him. His large frame walks around the front of the car, and when he gets in, his cologne sends butterflies erupting in my stomach. I wave away the unwanted attraction. I don't want this. I don't want to be going to church or anywhere with him.

I had hoped that I would not be picked as his bride, but that hope was squashed when I got the message that he would like me to attend Sunday church with him. I had been quiet when we first met; I even stuttered. I had thought that would make him not want me. It was small things that I hoped he didn't pick me for, so when my parents found out, they would know I was obedient, but I just wasn't his taste.

Amira was stunning, and when he hadn't gotten her involved in our first meeting, I had thought maybe he favored her more than myself and Selene, like boys are always mean to girls they fancy. I glance at Diarmuid. He is a far cry from a boy. He's a man and one who clearly knows his power.

I'm wondering if he thought I was easy prey. That maybe, I would be so alone with him. My stomach churns again at the thought.

"How has your week been?" Diarmuid's voice pulls me out of my musing.

"Very well, thank you, and yours?" I ask.

"Interesting," he states as we leave my family estate. His voice holds disinterest. I'm not one for making small talk, but I know for my parents' sake, I need to make some kind of an effort. Everything will be reported back to them.

"It was very kind of you to pick me up," I say politely.

He takes a quick look at me like he's seeing me for the first time. A smile plays on his lips but doesn't form.

"My pleasure."

"It's a beautiful day," I say and focus out the window. We can't get to the church quickly enough. He shifts gears, and the car moves faster like he wishes this ride to end as much as I do.

"I'm sure it will rain at some point today."

I continue with the small talk until Diarmuid starts to shift, like he can't take another second of this. Maybe this isn't a bad thing. He slows down and takes a left-hand turn into the grounds of the churchyard. It's lined with high-powered cars. This mass will only be open to people with an invite.

He pulls into a reserved parking spot and turns off the engine.

He doesn't speak as he gets out, and I stay where I am until he opens my door. I thank him and climb out. I only have a moment to breathe when the junior priest walks with a quick gait over to Diarmuid and takes his hand, shaking it several times. "Fantastic to see you at service, Mr. O'Sullivan."

Diarmuid removes his hand from the priest. "I'm looking forward to the service." Diarmuid makes it sound as though he's dead bored of everything. He reaches over and touches the small of my back, sending my spine into a tense straightness. If he notices the tension, he doesn't show it as he walks me to the door, where two more junior priests wait and shake Diarmuid's hand before we are led to our seats. Only then does Diarmuid take his hand off my back. We are fashionably late, and the church is full. Only a moment after we are seated, the mass starts.

Victor, who I know of, walks out onto the altar. Diarmuid tenses beside me, his jaw growing tight, but it's like a flash of silver when a fish surfaces in the ocean. And like that fish, it buries itself swiftly back into the darkness of the water. The tension is gone, and I'm left wondering if it even existed in the first place.

Victor. He's in his late fifties or early sixties. His hair is gray, black, and white, the gray mostly brushing the sides which are turning gray with age. He has heavy-lidded eyes that look both sincere and stern. He is a perfect man of the cloth—exactly what I would expect an old-world priest to look like.

Why would a man of the cloth make him uncomfortable? Recently, I've been educated about the world I might be marrying into. My parents wanted me to be Diarmuid O'Sullivan's bride so they could gain access to this world. Being part of this world means being controlled by priests like Victor.

Everyone kneels, and I move to do so, a step behind everyone; my mind is reeling. Diarmuid stares straight ahead, his disapproval unclear.

The O'Sullivans, too, are dangerous. In the late 1800s, they were announced as a mafia family. I shiver at that, just like I had done when my father educated me late into the night about the family I may be joining. Right now, the O'Sullivans claim that era is over for them. I take another peek at Diarmuid as we rise to join in the prayer, that I don't know the words to. Maybe they only declared they are no longer mafia as they are currently running for a position in the Dail Eireann, a political party who makes decisions with the people of Ireland as their interest. Most of their decisions are based on greed and climbing higher up the social ladder. My father said that one of them may be destined to be the president of Ireland.

We kneel again, and I'm glad when the service ends. Everyone files out and bends their knee to the altar before leaving. Once again, I'm grateful for my poise and manage to genuflect easily.

While I walk down the middle aisle, Diarmuid's hand finds the small of my back again. For the first time, I'm aware of so many people watching us. We stop at the exit as Victor himself shakes hands with the departing patrons. Diarmuid's fingers stiffen on my back, but his other hand encases Victor's, and they shake.

"Thank you for coming," Victor says, releasing Diarmuid's hand.

"It was my pleasure." Diarmuid's words are polite, a complete contradiction to the pressing fingers into my back. Victor's attention swivels to the next family as we leave the church. I'm very aware of how I am somehow invisible to these men. I don't mind, and to be fair, I'd prefer to go unnoticed. Diarmuid doesn't take his hand off my back until he opens the car door for me.

"That was a beautiful service." My voice is chirpy, not because I thought the service was good but because I survived my first outing, and the idea of getting home and maybe taking a swim makes me smile.

Diarmuid doesn't smile. "There is a map in the glove box." He juts his chin forward, his eyes focused on the glove box.

Okay. I open the glove box and take out the small map that has many grid lines crisscrossing it, and making it impossible to read.

I hand it to Diarmuid. He opens the map, and a small, cream-colored piece of heavy paper falls out. I glance at the paper and see what seems to be coordinates. Diarmuid runs his finger along the map, glancing at the scrap of paper before he taps the map twice.

"You can put that back." He tucks the paper into the map and hands it back to me. I've placed it back in its home when he reverses out of the churchyard. He doesn't say where we are going, but it isn't my home. I slouch in the seat but then remember that while he might have his eyes on the road, he is surely aware of my every move.

I open my clutch and take out some hand sanitizer, rubbing it on my hands. I'm tempted to offer some to Diarmuid but think twice and place it in my bag, which

I leave sitting on my lap. I exhale at the thought of not going home.

"Are you bored?" Diarmuid asks.

Shit.

I glance at him, and a smirk plays at his kissable lips. "No."

"If you are having trouble occupying yourself, you are more than welcome to pleasure me."

My heart thumps in my chest. I'm wondering if I heard him wrong, but I know I didn't. "I... I..." I have no idea how to respond. I don't want to pleasure him, but I also know I must do as he commands.

When a low laugh bubbles from his chest, my cheeks heat.

"You see, Niamh Connolly, I could make you do it." His laughter is gone. "I won't, but I could. Remember that."

I nod, just glad that I don't have to pleasure him. I know I won't always be as lucky. But today, I'll count my blessings.

We both remain silent. Diarmuid starts to slow the car down at an abandoned house in the Stepaside area. He comes to a complete halt. He leans closer to me, but his attention is out the window, as he points to a rusty old mailbox. "Will you retrieve the parcel from that mailbox?" He's parked along the sidewalk on my side.

I unclip my belt, happy to get out and take in some fresh air. The mailbox doesn't look like it's been used, so I don't expect to find anything in it. But a manila envelope held tightly shut by packing twine sits in the center. I turn to find Diarmuid watching me, and I raise the envelope to show him I got it and climb back into the car. When I hand it to him, I'm expecting him to open it, but he places it in the console between us.

We are silent again, but he's driving in the direction of my home, thank God.

"How do you feel, Niamh, about becoming an accessory?"

His words startle me, and I look from the passing scenery to Diarmuid. "Accessory to what?"

Diarmuid glances down at the envelope before his gray eyes land on me for a moment, sending a shiver racing down my spine. He refocuses on the road as he speaks. "Victor Madigan is the unholy priest of Dublin, my bride. In the envelope is the name and location of a person I have been commanded to kill, and that, my dear, is why we had to attend church." He pauses. "You're just here to look pretty."

CHAPTER FIVE
DIARMUID

Hands of the Kings Edict Three

> *The order will perform its duties to humanity, regardless of the laws of nations and average men. Kings are above all other men.*

I CAN'T SETTLE MYSELF. It's an odd feeling for me. So, it sends a thrill through me that I must be on the lookout for a threat. And there is a threat. I've never been the mouse in a cat chase, always the cat instead, so the role intrigues me.

As I pull into the public garage, I see Lorcan's and Ronan's high-powered cars. They're parked six cars apart, and I pull into a distant spot, ensuring we've all hidden our vehicles among the older models. We'd be far more noticeable if we parked side by side.

Stepping out of the fluorescent-lit garage, I look left and right before I start to walk.

A woman across the road walks her dog; she glances at me but quickly looks away while dipping her head. I don't sense danger from her, but she appears to feel it from me. That is wise.

It's a great instinct to have. We all have it; just most people fob it off as paranoia. I never ignore any gut feeling. I'll kill on instinct, and it never fails me.

I've been bred to kill; it wasn't exactly my first choice. But Victor saw a killer when I was a kid and made me into one. The training I received was some of the most intense and definitely not any kind of UN-sanctioned training in existence. What Victor made me do from a young age had turned me into the killing machine he needed, and I did it without question.

But I wanted more. I wanted to rule. I could be a King. But I couldn't say no to Victor—no one could.

I enter the "Church." A fitting name for the bar where I know my brothers await my arrival.

It's not the only property in the building. It acts as a multipurpose structure. A gold plaque beside the elevator lists the businesses here and which floor they are on. A doctor's office and hair salon are on the second floor. The first floor is occupied by a pet store, and the third floor is a tax agent. I'm going to none of them.

The key that I scoop out of my pocket presses into my palm as I hit the silver button on the elevator in the entry hall. Stepping in, I wait until the door closes before inserting my key into the elevator panel. The elevator shows the main floor, a few upper floors, and a basement level. The elevator goes two stories underground, one story farther than it is supposed to go. I turn the key fully, and the elevator starts to move.

We had modified the panel so that only our families' keys will take us to the final level of the building.

The elevator doors open to reveal a white brick wall with a single door in the center. I pull my key out of the elevator panel and place it securely in my pocket before I produce another key that slots into the door in front of me. The door opens to a semi-lit underground bar. There is a main room and several more private areas branching off. This is the throbbing heart of the O'Sullivans' enterprises. We were all sent into different ventures for the sake of the family, but everything comes back to the Church. Business deals, buying one-night companions, meeting political rivals—everything happens at the most exclusive bar in the country: The Church.

"Hello, Brother." Lorcan greets me with a wide smile that I don't return, but this doesn't faze him. Lorcan is the face of our political empire, and smiling and appearing friendly is part of his job that he never shakes off. He's almost animated in his greeting. It's always good for a mafia enterprise to have people entrenched in whatever political party we need to control, and Lorcan has been molded to perfection for the role.

Behind the smile is a man as equally dangerous as I am. Lorcan leads the way to a back table that has been partitioned off for privacy.

Ronan is already seated at the table. I knew he would be here, but the sight of my younger brother sends my fingers curling into fists; I grin at him, remembering how it felt to slam them into his face. Ronan picks up his drink and raises it at me as I take my seat. The fight we had was deeper than the excuse we gave everyone.

We said it was over a woman, but we never squabble about women; we never have to. They are always there at our disposal.

No. It was over who would rule.

Whispers that Ronan would be the leader of the O'Sullivan family didn't sit right with me as he is the youngest. The right passes first to Lorcan, who doesn't mind as he may lead Ireland one day, then to Wolf, who, in my opinion, doesn't deserve to lead a pack of wild dogs, nevermind people, and then to myself, who has been placed in a box by the Hand of the King, one that I want to get out of, but it's not looking great for me.

Lorcan sits across from me, and the waiter arrives to take our orders. Lorcan orders vodka straight, and I opt for a coffee. Both brothers look at me curiously, but I don't explain why I'm not drinking alcohol. I have a job after this, one that will require me to be clear-headed.

"Everything is looking great for us." Ronan kicks off the meeting. He is responsible for gaining legal sources of income for the family, with part of it going to the "Hand of the Kings," of course.

"My political party is a favorite right now, so I will make it into Dail Eireann and then on up." Our drinks arrive, and Lorcan takes a sip with a smile. "To ruling," he says, Ronan joins in with our brother's positivity.

I don't.

Both of my brothers look at me. Both with the same gray eyes, and dark hair, and dark suits. We are built similarly, but our rearing was all different.

Lorcan wasn't around Ronan and me much growing up, as he spent most of his time in a prestigious boarding school being educated on how to rule Ireland one day. That day seems to be growing closer and closer.

"I've made several deals on the black market for weapons, both in Ireland and the mainland of Britain," I say. Our enterprise is untouchable.

Just like us.

Ronan nods, and he leans closer on the table. "What have you found out about Andrew?"

I sit back in my seat and grin. "If you had showed up to the meeting, you would know."

Ronan glances at Lorcan before he speaks. "We arrived as soon as we could, but you, brother, were already gone. We will have a chance to speak at the annual Diners of Influence party."

Another outing. Great.

"I know about the event. I've been commanded to go with my brides."

Ronan smiles. "I'd like to get a good look at these brides of yours."

I release my cup of coffee before the porcelain cracks under my tightening fingers. "I will take your eyes out if you do," I say.

Ronan laughs, but there is no humor there.

"Now, no need for that. Ronan, you are going to get your chance soon." Lorcan says, always the politician.

Ronan shrugs. "You may be next. Doesn't it look better for your constituents if you are married? Aren't you into your image? Bleached teeth. Kissing babies and shit." Ronan doesn't know when to stop. His mouth has a way of running away with itself.

"You mock me, but having someone in the family in the upper tiers of government will open up avenues for our family that we couldn't even dream of ten years ago." Lorcan fires back in his defense. He's been brainwashed into thinking this is beneficial for just our family.

"You won't be benefiting our family. You are a stooge for Victor," I say.

Lorcan glares at me. The beast rises inside him. We all have it, but he controls it the best. He has to. "Our alliance with the Hands of Kings has given our family power like it hasn't had since Interpol started getting on our asses." Lorcan defends them.

I know I should stop, but I can't. Having Ronan across from me giving me a smug smile that I want to wipe off his face has me continuing.

"I'm not seeing it. Everything we do is for *them*." Bitterness I had thought was deeply buried, raises its head. It's my next job that is bothering me more than anything I have been asked to do before. I've never questioned a kill, but this time is different.

"Careful, little brother. It isn't wise to question my loyalty to me and mine." Lorcan states.

"You seem to be paranoid, Diarmuid. Are you experiencing some disloyalty with your new swines?"

I rise, having listened to enough of Ronan's shit. Lorcan places a hand on my arm. "Sit, Brother." He glances around like someone might be watching.

I don't sit because of that; I sit because I know hitting Ronan once wouldn't satisfy me, and I'm not sure I'd stop.

Ronan grins like he has won.

"So, what was the news about Andrew?" Lorcan swings back to his earlier question.

"He was found dead three weeks ago, a woman's body laid upon his shallow grave."

I pick up my coffee and take a long sip. Shutting my brain down, not thinking about how I killed him, how nobody but the person who laid the body there knows. No one can ever know.

"Who was the woman?" Ronan asks.

I place the cup carefully back on the saucer. "They didn't say. A page delivered the news."

"Why?" Lorcan asks.

"Security reasons," I answer and watch both my brothers.

Ronan grins like this is a game. "They thought the killer was in the room." Bingo. He's right.

I shrug. "They didn't say."

He tuts. "It's clear as mud, Diarmuid. It's served me well to have Andrew out of the way, so I won't pine over him."

"Careful, Brother, you sound like you might have had a hand in his death." It's my turn to smirk.

He grits his teeth and then relaxes. "I'm looking forward to seeing your brides."

I don't know my brides well, but they are my brides, and Ronan better not push me.

"Ronan, show some respect," Lorcan states.

Any man who touches what is mine won't live long enough to brag about it. I make that promise through narrowed eyes at Ronan. It's a good thing that I am supposed to be meeting with my brides tonight. I need to let out some tension. I hope Niamh wears her church dress; it would be my pleasure to destroy it. After a bit more speculation about Andrew, I depart. I must do my job. Duty always calls.

I sit in my car, adjacent to the front door of the school. The graffiti on the wall next to me reads "Stey in Skool." I touch the envelope in my lap, the envelope that contains the identity of the person I am supposed to kill.

I open it again and glance at the picture. It's not a shady-looking teacher or the stern headmaster. I'm looking into the blue eyes of a young boy, Brien Cahill. He is eight. The son of Kane Cahill. Victor wants to hurt Kane, so Brien must die. That's my order. I've never disobeyed an order, but Brien isn't the guilty party here.

Why should sons pay for their father's sins?

I stare at the picture, brain spinning. When I was Brien's age, I made my first kill; Victor made me finish off one of his hits. I hesitated. Victor and Andrew punished me for this later when they found out I shivered and cried. I never hesitated again.

I place the image of the boy back in the envelope when movement along the sidewalk catches my eye. Brien meets two people, who I assume are his parents, and the three walk down the road together. I wait until the family is almost out of sight before I follow them all the way to the church. They enter, and I step onto holy ground only a moment later.

The church is deserted at this hour, and I take a seat at the back. I watch as the parents kneel to pray. I assume the man is Kane. His belly rolls out over his trousers; he's obviously well fed. The strain on his shirt buttons is unappealing to the eye, but his wife still looks up at him with love in her eyes. Love can be blind. In this case, you would be better off having no sight.

The boy runs a fire engine toy along the top of the pew. I could follow them home and wait until the boy's mother starts dinner. While Brien is playing in the yard, I could snatch him, and make him disappear. Kane wouldn't be fit enough to catch me with all that extra cushion.

That's what I could do. Instead, I watch as a priest walks to the family with a bucket and a mop. Brien tucks his toy in his backpack and takes the bucket without question. The priest smiles fondly at the boy and rubs his hair before speaking to Brien's parents.

Of course. Nothing looks better on a college application than a lifetime of volunteer work. This boy has a planned future.

One that I am supposed to take away.

I rise from my seat and walk up the center aisle. The priest glances my way and smiles. When I reach him, he holds out his hand. "Welcome. You are new to our church? I'm Isaac Waryn."

I don't take the priest's outstretched hand. The boy is far enough away not to hear as he mops the mosaic floor of the church.

"We need to talk." I glance at Brien's parents.

I look at Kane, who has paled. "You are Diarmuid O'Sullivan."

I nod. "Yes, I am, Kane."

I don't turn to the priest as I speak to him but keep my gaze fixed on Kane in case he decides to run.

"Father, close the main doors." The priest doesn't act, but Brien's father nods while he swallows. "Do as he says."

The priest doesn't look happy but closes the main church doors. I take a seat behind the couple, and they turn to look at me.

"What is this about?" The wife asks.

"A hit has been placed on Brien's head," I say.

The mother's wild eyes seek her son out as the priest returns.

But I'm focused on Kane. "Why would that be?" I ask him. I know why, but I want to hear it from his miserable lips.

"A gambling debt, I can assume," he says.

The wife starts to rise, appalled at her husband.

"Sit down," I warn her. She slowly does, but not before checking to make sure her son is still there.

The priest stands and watches me, not with fear but disgust.

"I'm the hitman," I say, so they understand the gravity of the situation.

"You will not harm that boy in the house of God." Isaac, the priest, grips his rosary beads like they would save the boy. If I wanted Brien dead, he would be dead.

"I won't, Father, that's why I'm sitting here telling you this."

I glance at Kane. "I don't think a son should pay for his father's incompetence," I say through gritted teeth. Every father figure I had never showed a shred of goodness.

Maybe this is why I got this job. To save someone from a future like mine.

"Brien needs to be sent to relatives in the United States," I say, and the mother covers her mouth, tears pouring onto her hand. Her husband reaches out to comfort her, but she moves away and glares at him.

Good.

"You will have a closed-casket funeral," I inform the priest who sits across from us like the weight of my words are resting on his frail shoulders.

I will try, and hide it the best I can from the authorities. I know this is a huge risk, but I won't take the life of a child. I can't say no to Victor, so this is the only way. I have my own people with the police, but Victor doesn't let anyone know all of the members of the Hand of Kings. One of the authorities could be one of Victor's men, another risk I'll have to take.

"Your sister lives in Texas," The father says.

The wife glares at him again but looks at me. "Can't you renegotiate? We have money," she says and then pauses. "You spent it all, didn't you?" The accusation causes her husband's face to darken.

"This is no place to air our dirty laundry."

Her hand connects with her husband's face. "You brought this down on your son's head."

"This is the only way it can be," I say.

The priest nods. "I can organize a closed casket. He glances at Brien, who is oblivious to how his life is about to change.

I never have sympathy in these matters, but the mother's devastation is bringing out my softer side. I want to offer her comfort, but I don't have much to give.

"You must wait at least a year before following your son to the United States." The mother's sobs grow, but she nods.

The priest looks upon them with shock and sympathy, but he is also scared, and I need to lean into their fear so they do exactly what I say.

"If you don't do as I say, someone else will come to kill Brien, and trust me, they will do it."

I rise from my seat and stare down at Kane. "Walk me to the door," I tell him.

He's afraid, his tail between his legs as he numbly walks toward the main doors. Once we reach the small porch, I stop and look at the man who has done this to his son.

My fist connects with his face. His nose cracks under the weight of the punch, and he cries out, but I cover his mouth with my hand.

"Swallow that fucking pain, you piece of shit. If I hear of you gambling one more cent, I'll come and kill you myself." Blood from his nose soaks my hand. "I won't make it quick. Trust me." His eyes widen, and I release him, leaving the church.

I am so tired of parents who don't think about their kids.

CHAPTER SIX

SELENE

PLEASURE. SUCH A SMALL word but one I can't find in the one-hundred-word crossword puzzle. A cup of tea that had been piping hot when I started has cooled in the mug. I swallow the liquid and continue my search. I have only two more words to find, and it will be complete.

A groan from my grandfather has me glancing at him.

"You know the rules. I intended on finishing off that puzzle." He slips a small pair of glasses from the breast pocket of his navy shirt and places them on his nose. He stands over me to see how much I have completed.

I continue my search as I speak. "I know the rules. You have twenty-four hours to complete it before I get in." And his twenty-four hours are up.

"Well, the new newspaper hasn't been delivered yet, so you are doing the puzzle early."

With my eyes still glued to the puzzle, I point to the newspaper at the end of the dining table with my pencil. "Your new newspaper is there." I hadn't broken our golden rule. He steps away from me and removes his glasses. I hide a smile as I watch him leave the room.

A large arch joins the dining room with the kitchen. The kettle buzzes away as he clicks it on.

Found it. I circle the word and move on to the final one. I can smell pudding and hear the microwave come to life.

"You know Grandmother doesn't like her pudding microwaved." I smile softly as my grandfather tuts again.

"It's a good thing it's only for me," he says as he re-enters the dining room with his small timer. He pauses at my shoulder and reads the word I'm looking for. "Hmmm," he says but continues to his side of the table and sets up his newspaper, opening it up to the puzzle page.

He only gets the papers for the puzzle. I told him so many times that he could buy a puzzle book as he doesn't read anything else in the paper, but he likes the newspaper and not the small booklet of puzzles.

The microwave still hums in the background as he takes a seat at the head of the old mahogany table. It has some secret drawers that I loved playing with as a kid. I had found the panel when I was coloring under the table on a stormy night. Whenever we had thunder and lightning, my grandmother would make me hide under the table with a flashlight and tell me to color. One particular night, the storm raged for longer than normal, and I got bored of coloring, so I started to touch the table and discovered the secret drawers. Old twine, a pair of scissors, and some clippings of newspapers were all I found. To me, they were treasures.

"I ran into your parents yesterday," he says, and I look up from the crossword puzzle, leaving my memories behind.

"Let me guess…they didn't ask about me." I know the answer already; it should stop hurting after all this time, but I still feel the twinge in my gut at how they don't care.

"No, they didn't," he says. He is never one to sugarcoat things, and I love that about him.

I'm tempted to return to my puzzle but can see in my grandfather's deep brown eyes that he isn't finished talking. I take another sip of my cold tea and regret the decision straight away.

"I know that your mother is my child, but I promise I won't play favorites."

"If you did that, I would be the winner." I smile at him.

"Yes, very true. I just meant that you could tell me about this tiff that has separated you from your parents."

I don't want to talk about it, and it peeves me that I always have to be the one to explain what happened with them.

I don't, of course. How can I tell my grandparents that I only exist to be married off? Discovering that at the age of sixteen was life altering, to say the least. I'd had everything as an only child and could do anything I wanted. A picture-perfect childhood until the reality of what my future would be destroyed it all for me.

I won't be the one to destroy my grandparents' world. They would object, but doing so would only cause a rift within our family, and I'd still have to marry. They loved their daughter, and I didn't want to put my mother in a bad light with them.

"You will need to ask them about that," I finally say.

"I did, and they wouldn't answer. That's why I'm asking you." Of course, he did. He hates to see me separated from my parents even though I've lived with my grandparents for years. Simply saying that my parents traveled a lot, and I wanted company or making the excuse that my mother and I didn't get along has worked for the past few years, but I know the older I get, and my parent's cold response to me, makes my grandparents question this arrangement all the more.

"Móraí, you know I'm not an idiot. If I am not speaking to my parents, there is a good reason."

His eyes soften, "I guess I can trust that reasoning."
    "You can," I answer just as the doorbell rings.
    I rise at the same time as my grandfather, but my grandmother calls out to us. "I'll get it." We both sit back down, and I focus on finding the final word. I can hear the low, distant hum of conversation at the door. Grandfather gets up as the microwave beeps to let him know his pudding is ready for consumption. When the talking ceases, my grandmother enters the dining room with an envelope in her hand.
    She looks so much like my mother; only there is kindness and laugh lines on her face, whereas, my mother's is perfect due to all the Botox she has had over the years.
    "It's for you, dear." She hands over the envelope, and my stomach tightens. I recognize the seal instantly. I force a smile and get up, the puzzle forgotten.
    "I'd better get ready for the day." I press a quick kiss to her rosy and freshly washed cheek and clutch the envelope to my chest.
    "Will you be back for dinner?" she asks, her gaze darting to the envelope that she is curious about.

"I'll try." I press a second kiss to her cheek and inhale the scent of her moisturizer.

"Bye, Grandfather," I call.

"See you later, love. I'll have this new puzzle done in no time," he shouts back from the kitchen.

My grandmother purses her lips and shakes her head. I laugh. "Twenty-four hours, Grandfather," I remind him and leave.

I walk outside and across the small space to the apartment that my grandparents had converted for me above a detached garage. I didn't mind staying in their home, but they believed a lady my age needed her own space. Their kindness never ceases to amaze me.

I climb the stairs and enter my apartment, which is always unlocked. I told my grandparents they could come in whenever they wanted, but they always knocked and never entered unless I told them they could.

I smile at how lucky I am to have them.

The apartment is cozy and always warm. It's a bit of a sun trap. I appreciate the Velux windows that line the roof, allowing all the sunshine to pour in.

The small two-seater couch is scattered with cushions that my grandmother and I knitted over time. I love each one of them.

Stopping at my small kitchen table, I sit down and turn the thick envelope over, breaking the seal. I allow the contents to fall out, already knowing what it is.

Birth control.

Three months ago, these deliveries began. Part of my agreement with the Hand of Kings is to make certain that no unexpected princes are created. Tonight, I have to go to the house. To perform my duties, duties that I was born to perform. I've had years to let this knowledge sink in, but it never did until now. This is the destiny my parents decided for me before I was even born. It was the only reason I was born.

I was sixteen when they sat me down. I'll never forget my mother's cold exterior. They gave me everything but never affection. I never craved it, as my grandparents filled that void. I never understood why there was no "I love you" at bedtime. No morning hugs. I just assumed that's how parents were with their kids. They were not our friends, but our parents. But it ran so much deeper than that. They literally had me so I could be raised to fill a role that terrified me.

"You are old enough now for us to tell you about your future." My father had started. There was a nervous energy in the room. That energy was mine, but at the time, I couldn't pinpoint it.

"Okay," I responded. Was this the part where I got serious about my future? Would they push me into politics or law? But I nodded, ready to hear what path had been laid out before me.

"The O'Sullivan family have just given us great news." My father glanced at my mother, and for the first time, she smiled with real delight.

I'd never heard of the family and at the time wondered if they owned a firm or some business.

"You will be a bride to Diarmuid O'Sullivan." My father had said while looking back at me, but the smile he shared with my mother was gone.

"A bride?" Confusion at their words had me squirming in my seat.

My father shuffled further in his seat. "Yes, he will have three to select from, and we know he will pick you."

"What if I don't want to be a bride?" What sixteen-year-old thought about marriage? I know I didn't. My dreams were further from that path than they could ever imagine.

My mother spoke this time. "It's not about what you want, dear; it is what is going to happen. Don't get awkward. It's already been agreed upon." She seemed agitated.

"No." I shook my head.

My father rises and walks to the fireplace. "Like your mother said, it's already been agreed upon, and you don't say no to these people."

His words were deadly. These people? *"I don't understand."*

My mother rose and joined my father at the fireplace. "You will be his bride when the time comes. You will obey him, and you will earn your place at his side. Make no mistake, Selene, there is no getting out of this."

They had left me alone, trembling, and I had run. Run to my grandparents, never revealing the real reason that I couldn't stay under my parents' roof.

The driver opens the car door for me, and I try not to gasp at the sprawling mansion before me. I've been brought up with wealth and have a healthy trust fund, but the sheer size of this place leaves my mind scrambling. I've already seen the Hand of the Kings' mansion, but it still takes my breath away for more reasons than one.

Its sheer size is intimidating, but I know what waits for me on the other side of the door. My first meeting with Diarmuid comes to my mind, when he made me touch myself in front of the other girls, and how he made Niamh touch my breasts, but the part that sent waves of pleasure coursing through me was when he helped me.

I've never had a man's hands on me. It was forbidden. Before I was sixteen, I had some stolen kisses, but that was it. I've never been touched. I hate how I liked Diarmuid's touch so much.

It's cold, and the breeze has me tightening my beige coat around me. I dressed for the autumn weather in warm pants, a cream polo neck jumper, and heavy black boots. My dark hair flows down my back, and I dip my head as I'm led into the hallways of the mansion. Our footsteps echo loudly as a wordless maid guides me through the house, and we don't stop until we arrive at double doors that open into a bedroom.

Amira and Niamh are already inside, and both of them look at me when I enter. Amira can't hide her disgust with me, but Niamh offers a warm, shy smile. I like her and can see kindness in her brown eyes. I wonder if she was introduced into this world the same way I was. Or if she always knew what she was.

Amira, on the other hand, has waves of hostility pouring off her. I try to ignore her as the maid closes the door behind me.

In the room is a large queen-size bed, and my stomach tightens. All of a sudden, I'm feeling hot and shrug out of my beige jacket.

Diarmuid is very attractive, more so than I could have hoped for, and I spent years trying to picture the man my parents handed me over to. His brother Lorcan was easy to find on the internet, as he is into politics, and his face is plastered across so many articles. He's extremely handsome, too, and after meeting Diarmuid, it is easy to see they are brothers.

No matter how attractive Diarmuid is, though, this entire arrangement is so off-putting to me. I feel like a farm animal being led to auction, and I don't know if I or that farm animal would be the better for winning.

I look around and place my coat on a chair where another one sits. I have no idea which girl it belongs to.

Awkwardness fills the room now. Amira folds her arms across her chest. A bold red paints her lips, and she raises a brow at me.

I don't like her at all.

The door opens, and we all shift our stances but relax when a maid enters. She doesn't speak but lays out three parcels all wrapped in deep green paper. Once she leaves, I walk to the bed and open the first one. What in God's name are these? They can't be called clothing. They would barely cover me, and the more intimate parts of the black underwear have Velcro that can be ripped open. The noise of pulling it apart is loud in the room. Amira's elbow rubs against me not so gently as she opens the second parcel. It's identical to the one I opened. She holds it up, and with a cruel smile in her gaze, she turns to me, stretching out the material.

"Hmmm. This one is kind of large. Might be for you." I don't take the garment, and she tosses it in my direction. It lands right beside my hand. I'm not heavy by any means, but I do have far more curves than Amira.

Amira opens the third one and holds it up. "This seems like it's my size. I can't picture either of you fitting in it." She grins and begins stripping out of her clothes, unfazed that she's naked in front of us.

I glance at Niamh, who looks uncomfortable. Amira slips into the bit of material and does a spin for us. "What do you think?" She smirks.

"Save that for Diarmuid. We're not interested," I snap, hating how she grins at us.

"How stupid of you. This is a competition." Amira walks to a full-length mirror and assesses herself.

"If you say so," I remark, and my fingers toy with the undergarment. I am not shy, but I won't parade myself before it's necessary.

"When you fail, I want you to remember what you are seeing right now. This is everything that you won't be." Amira spins from the mirror.

"If I remember correctly, Diarmuid left you to the side the last time," I bite back.

Amira marches to me with fire in her eyes. "Boys are always mean to the girls they want the most." She continues to the bed and picks up a set of silver bracelets that have a small hook on them. She slips them on. "I don't think he is into fat girls."

I bite my tongue, not wanting to argue, but she grates on my last nerve.

Amira looks at Niamh. "Dear God, you look petrified." She laughs. "He won't want something like you."

I spin toward Amira. "That's enough." I defend Niamh, as Niamh doesn't fight back.

I hate bullies.

"Or what?" Amira asks.

I don't answer her; I'm not the fighting type, but I also won't stand for her abuse. We are all here for the same reason and being cruel to one another isn't helping.

Niamh walks to the bed and picks up her own set of identical garments. Amira goes back to looking at herself in the mirror.

"Thank you," Niamh says gently.

I smile at her, but sadness pours into me. "You are welcome." I get a sense no one has ever defended Niamh. No matter the outcome of this, I make a promise to watch out for her.

I strip with my back to the girls and get into the underwear. Just like Amira, I slip on the bracelets. Robes I hadn't noticed are laid out at the top of the bed, and I pick up one, happy to cover up my skin. The silky material is cool against my flesh that has started to feel like it's burning. My bare feet sink into the cream carpet under my feet. Niamh quickly gets dressed and does the same as me, donning the robe.

When we are ready, Amira marches past us and puts hers on, too. She doesn't tie it but leaves it open.

"May the best girl win. I'm certain that's me." She grins.

I want to snap back at her, but the door opens for a third time, and the same maid that had led us here and brought in the garments looks at us all over. The stern look she has worn since our arrival doesn't leave her face. Her nose is pinched, her lips downturned. She wouldn't be getting employee of the month. There is no warmth in her green eyes.

"Follow me." Her lips barely move as she speaks. We file out of the room as she leads us all barefoot up another flight of stairs. We don't meet anyone, and I'm too focused on trying to settle my pounding heart to take in my surroundings.

She opens the third door on the left, and Amira pushes past and enters first. When we are all in the room, I pause. A metal pole is erected in the middle of the room. Off to the right, a wash station has been set up.

Niamh is frozen like a deer in headlights, and the maid roughly shoves Niamh forward and guides her to the pole. Amira is standing at the pole. The maid gives me a stern look, and I join the girls. There are chains dangling above our heads.

"Put your hands up." The maid barks like we are a bunch of disobedient toddlers.

Niamh raises her hands, and I watch as the maid loops chains through the small hole on our bracelets. Amira is next, and for the first time, fear shines in her gaze.

"I'm not putting my hands up there," she says.

I don't blame her; I'm not exactly excited to be chained like Niamh.

What I didn't expect was for the maid to slap Amira across the face. The sound of flesh hitting flesh makes me flinch.

I think Amira will attack the maid, but she surprises me by raising her hands. It is shocking to see how Amira acts like a kicked dog over this.

I raise my hands as I'm next, and once the maid has us all tied up, she goes back to Niamh and takes out black silk blindfolds from a fold in the front of her apron. She places a blindfold over Niamh's eyes. Next is Amira, who has a mark on her face but doesn't object this time. When the maid stops at me, I dip my head, but my mind is reeling. What the hell is this for?

The last thing that I see is the stern look on the maid's face before my world turns black, and I'm left dangling with the other brides as we wait for what is next.

CHAPTER SEVEN

AMIRA

M Y FACE BURNS ALONG with my skin. I want to lash out; I want to hurt someone—the maid, maybe, for putting her hands on me. The moment her hand had struck my face, I was back home with my mother, knowing answering back or retaliating would lead to something far worse. The maid had hit me right on the spot where my mother's hand had struck, and I ached to touch my face.

I pull against the chains, and they rattle. I hear a large intake of breath, most likely from Niamh, who hangs beside me. Is she also thinking of how the maid had hurt me?

Humiliation makes me hot. Shame hammers through my system. I should have hit the maid back; she had struck me in front of the other two, who already thought they were better than me. I had seen the look on Selene's face; pity had filled her gaze. I didn't want her pity; I wanted her gone from here with her smart mouth.

I vow, as I yank against my chains, that the next time the maid touches me, I will claw into her and won't stop. I release more anger on the chains, but they are tight, and I don't get any release.

My mother hit me so much, but I could control myself. She never struck me in front of people and definitely not two girls who were out to get me. They are already teaming up against me. But they don't know how strong I am. I will myself to stay still and try out a smile.

It's all right. The next time I come across that maid, she will wish she had never laid a finger on me.

I stop my musing when I hear the door open. It closes with a soft click. I can't see, and I am tempted to rub my blindfold against my shoulder to see who has entered. My other senses kick in; I can smell him. His cologne brings me back to that first meeting with him. Seeing him walk into the room, watching him instruct the other girls to touch each other. He had left me out once, not this time. I lick my red-painted lips and relax my mouth. I want to smile but tell myself I'll appear too eager, so I keep my lips slightly parted in what I can picture as a sensual manner.

His footsteps are slow, and my body comes alive, wondering what he will do. Will he touch me? I grow moist between my legs at the mere thought.

He walks again, and the air seems to shift as he moves. A breeze brushes my navel, I left my robe open intentionally to entice him. It must be working. A sense of disappointment rushes as his footsteps echo past me, but not before I inhale him deeply.

Silence grows, and then I hear a whimper. It's Niamh; I'd recognize her voice anywhere. She whimpers again, and the shuffle of clothes has me tightening my thighs together, making my chains rattle. A slurping sound has me tingling, and then Niamh's whimpers turn to moans.

I want to shift again; I want it to be my turn. I imagine him with her legs spread, his handsome face buried between them, tasting her. He will taste us all like wine;only I will be the finest. I've shaved my pussy and used some rose-scented shower gel just for him.

The waiting is sending me forward, and my chains rattle again as Niamh continues to moan, and the slurping sound doesn't stop; it only grows faster and louder. Is he using only his mouth or his fingers, too? I want to see what is happening so badly.

I want him to do to me whatever it is that is making her cry out in ecstasy. I tighten my thighs again as she continues to cry out until her moans turn to shudders and the lapping sound ceases.

Diarmuid's footsteps grow close to me, and I spread my legs, letting him know I'm ready and want him, but once again, he walks past.

I hear water splashing and think of the wash station I had seen set up in the corner of the room.

It's agony waiting. *Please let me be next.* But once again, the scent of his cologne flutters past me in a teasing breeze. I get a whiff, and then he's gone.

Selene's breathing grows harsh, and I know he's moved onto her.

She isn't as loud as Niamh, and I don't hear any slurping, so I'm not sure what he is doing to her. But her rushed breaths turned to groans like she's trying to keep them in but can't any longer. Who could? I can assume that Diarmuid is a man who knows exactly what a woman wants. My breasts swell with need. I'm soaking, and I know the mere touch from him would have me releasing the agony between my legs.

It feels like an eternity until he pauses in front of me. I'm pushing against the restraints, yearning for his touch. And I get what I want. A large hand slides between my parted thighs and stops at my soaking, throbbing core. I inhale a sharp breath as he touches my clitoris. His breath brushes my cheek, and I throw my head back and let out a moan as he slips one finger inside me. I've never had any other fingers, only my own, inside me, and this is so much better than I could have dreamed of. A second finger enters, my head shoots up, and the pressure inside my walls grows around his fingers. I push myself down on his hand, wanting more. I moan into his face. His hand lands close to my chin before it trails up to my cheek, and he pauses. I want to scream at him. *Don't stop…*I'm so close to coming, but he removes his fingers and then proceeds to remove my mask. I blink several times at the light before his face comes into view. He's far more handsome up close, his jawline so strong, and his lips are red and swollen. His finger prods my face, and I recoil.

I glance at the other two girls, who still have their blindfolds on. Why has he gone off-script with me? I want to beg him to continue.

His finger circles the ache in my cheek.

"Who did this?"

The slap the maid gave me must have left a mark. I'm sure it's worse since my mother got there first with her own slap.

"The maid," I whisper, looking into gray eyes of steel. "She slapped me."

He nods once; his features appear carved from stone. I'm surprised when he reaches up and undoes my chains. Does that mean this ends? I won't get to come? I want to say something to him but let my hands hang at my side; as with professional efficiency, Diarmuid releases the other two girls, also.

I watch as he strides across the room like an angel who just escaped Hell. He's beautiful but deadly, dressed all in black. He disappears through the door, but I still yearn for his touch. I find myself stumbling after him.

"Do not follow him," Selene warns, but she doesn't understand. It was different with me; he removed my blindfold and not theirs. So, there is more to Diarmuid and me than them. I leave the room and race to the balcony that looks down on the second floor, where a commotion has broken out.

He approaches the maid with slow, controlled steps, but the rise and fall of his shoulders is a warning that he's angry. His guards stand along the wall, their gazes fixed ahead.

"You put your hands on one of my brides?" He questions, but before she can gather her courage to respond, he holds two fingers up, silencing her.

"I should have your hands for that." His statement is so off-hand, yet it sends a deadly thrill down my spine.

"Or maybe your life." He tilts his head like he's really thinking about doing just that.

The maid no longer has that stern look on her face; she appears shaken to the core. I don't know what has her looking up, but her gaze clashes with mine, and I grin.

"Take her out back." Diarmuid addresses one of his guards, who moves toward the maid. I lean over the rail to see what will happen next.

"It's your choice; he will take your hands or your life." The guard grips her by the arm, and she starts to plead, but there is no forgiveness shown for what she just did.

"NO ONE touches them. No one. This is your only warning. I don't care who you are. I will kill you." His anger swirls and grows, yet his voice is low. Deadly. I clutch my heart in joy that brings tears to my eyes. He's protecting me.

I've never felt more powerful as I walk back to the room where Selene and Niamh are waiting with their robes back in place.

I grin at them but don't tell them what just happened. They will have to ask nicely first.

This is exactly the kind of man I need in my life. I have to win his heart, and I will.

CHAPTER EIGHT

DIARMUID

Hands of the Kings Edict Four
Kings are made to lead our world, and they must also lead their homes. Kings are required to take on a Consort. Three candidates (Brides) are chosen for the examination, exploration, and exploitation of the King. One will be chosen as his Consort.

T HE TASTING DID LITTLE to satisfy me. On the contrary, I find myself wanting more. Needing more. Every shiver and reaction from them had sent a thrill to my cock. I want to take each of them one at a time or all together. Each of them was exquisite. Choosing just one is proving to be a problem. If only I could keep them all…but I know that is against the rules.

The churchyard that I drive into is deserted. But that doesn't fool me; I know from the moment I pass the large wrought iron gates and move down the long, winding driveway that I am being watched.

St. Gertrude's church is the perfect location for a man like Victor to hold his private meetings in. Who would suspect a man of such high standing in our society could be so calculated? Truly, a wolf in sheep's clothing.

Aren't we all? I muse as I park the car and get out. No service is happening, but several people mill about the sanctuary. If this truly was God's house, we would all combust into flames for our sins.

Even the people cleaning the church are Pages and Barons assigned to protect Victor with their lives. Even if someone successfully took out the priest, they wouldn't make it out of the building. Killing Victor meant killing yourself, which is the only reason the priest is still breathing. But a man can fantasize about ending Victor's life. His day will come, just not today, apparently.

I nod at the cleaners as I walk to the confessional boxes. There is a row of them at the back of the church. Each one has its red curtains closed. The one I select has a small, red light above the door, telling people it's occupied. It's my cue to enter this one. I step into the small box and draw the curtain behind me. I can hear a creak of wood from the other side and know Victor has been waiting for me.

I won't kneel as I make my confession. I never do.

"Bless me, Father, for I have sinned," I start.

"When did you sin?" Victor's voice is clear through the wood. I can't see him; I don't want to see his face.

He's asking me if the job was done. "Yesterday afternoon." I think of the boy whose life I was meant to take. He's on a plane heading for a new life in America. My stomach squirms when the mother's look of pure devastation enters my mind.

"With God as your witness?"

"My only witness," I respond. There is a long pause.

"You've done well, my son." Victor gives me his unwanted praise. More silence drags out.

I've always been sent to kill men, but a boy...I know it's wise for me to question it so as not to raise suspicion.

"I wonder if this kind of sin will happen again?" Basically, will I have to kill any more children?

"Not right now."

I glare at the wood that separates us. I can't see through it. It's not like in the movies when you can see the silhouette of the priest through the wooden partition with its small cutouts. This one is pretty much solid, with a few small holes to allow our voices to pass through.

But I don't need to see Victor in order to know what he is doing. He moves, and I hear the worn wood creak as the priest shifts his weight. The sound of the silky fabric of his robe against the rougher fabric of the seat is another noise I can hear. I can almost see Victor's nostrils flare as he lets out a deep breath. Is he annoyed at my line of questioning?

"This is your greatest sin."

"This sin surprised me, I admit with genuine emotion.

"You have done it all for the sake of a greater purpose, a greater world." Victor recites, and I detect no emotion in the old man's voice.

I roll my eyes at that. Brien Cahill's father had a gambling debt. With the wealth of the Hand of Kings, this could have been forgiven without affecting business at all. There was no greatness to this act. It was unnecessary. I bite my tongue, not saying what I truly want to say.

"Have you ever wondered why I didn't send you to boarding school like your brothers?" His voice is closer to the partition. It is something I had wondered. I am as intelligent as my brothers, yet Victor had sent me to run weapons and kill enemies, and now I've been lowered to killing children.

Once again, I seem incapable of answering.

"I plan to make all three O'Sullivan brothers Kings. Do you know why we need Kings, Diarmuid?" Victor doesn't seem put off by my silence.

I already know the answer to this because it has been drilled into my head repeatedly since I was a child. It was part of the plan: repeat the creed until the children believed nothing else. I didn't buy into everything they taught us; sometimes, I saw beyond the curtain that hides the greed, monsters, and madness.

"Yes." I finally answer.

"This world is filled with manmade wonders, ancient and modern. The greatest of these wonders exist only because the right person led an entire nation of people. These men didn't have to heed the whims of politicians. They didn't have to worry about maintaining face for an election. They only needed to obey themselves. They accomplished great feats. The human race was made in such a way that the majority of people are followers. They are made to bring to life the dreams of greater men. Whether through evolution or divine right, some men are just made to be Kings."

I roll my eyes again at his spiel. He loves the sound of his own voice as he spews his poison. Like we are still kids eager to please or terrified to fail.

"We put those Kings in the right places so that humanity can continue to achieve great things. Your brothers will be Kings like the other Kings I have made, but you...you are a once-in-a-generation type of King. You are my Warrior King."

He really loves to talk, and all he is doing is grating on my nerves. He's trying to praise me, so I don't think about the child he thinks I've just murdered. He continues to speak about my brothers and me as if he owns us. I can sense the weight of my gun in the band of my trousers. My fingers twitch. I can detect exactly where Victor is sitting. I could end it all.

"Richard the Lionheart, Alexander the Great, and Charlemagne. These were Warrior Kings, Diarmuid. Warrior Kings are made to fight the battles that turn the stomachs of other Kings. They are...special."

He must really detect my displeasure at killing the kid. He's never tried to praise me so much in one sitting. Is it panic that I hear in his voice? I think how one single bullet could fulfill every dream of revenge that has ever woken me from sleep. There are guards in the sanctuary, but none of them have my training. I could move quickly. I might be able to get away.

"When your father left us, I felt great sadness. He thought that your family could survive without the Kings. He didn't succeed. We didn't let him. When he came crawling back to us, I felt as if the universe had given me another chance to make a difference in this world. I hope that I didn't make a mistake."

All my thoughts cease. Something in Victor's tone has changed. Is it from my lack of response earlier?

I hear the crinkle of paper and wait to hear what he has to say.

"This is the autopsy of Andrew O'Sullivan. A curious document, if I may be honest. The head, hands, and feet have been removed. Without the use of DNA, the coroner may have never identified our dear Andrew. I will say that Andrew didn't have a peaceful exit from this world. One of his lungs was punctured. Ribs broken. Femur snapped. Burn marks on his chest. Obscenely brutal, his death. I imagine that whoever killed your uncle harbored a great deal of resentment toward him." I hide a smile at each one of the wounds I gave my uncle. Pride swells in my chest.

"This line of work does that to a man. You can throw a stone in any direction in Dublin and hit a man who wanted to kill my uncle," I reply.

"Yes, but their want would have never made them actually do the deed. No one is foolish enough to do this. Unless they felt they could get away with it," Victor responds.

I grit my teeth and then relax my jaw. "Obviously, they won't get away with it."

"I don't imagine they will. It's just strange. No one I know would have ever left a body like this in a grave; it would have been destroyed," Victor says simply.

"It sounds like they were stupid," I respond.

"Or that they wanted to have a grave to spit on."

He knows. He knows I did it; that's exactly why I gave my uncle a grave. So I could return to it and remember his brutal death. The way Victor is talking suggests he suspects me, but I don't think he is the one who set me up. He isn't the one who placed the female body on top of my uncle's grave.

"I know how you feel about me, my son. I know that one day, you will disregard your own life and take mine. I can see it in you. I just want you to realize that there are worse monsters than me."

My heart hammers at his confession. The creak of the wood and the flash of light tells me he is gone. I sit for a moment, listening, and when I step out of the confessional box, the movement of the cleaners catches my attention. They don't look at me, but I now know I was surrounded the entire time.

Victor is leaving no room for an attempt on his life.

As I walk out of the church, I realize I may have far more people watching me than I suspected.

CHAPTER NINE

NIAMH

T HE SEA IS CALM today. Waves crash along the shoreline, some race across the heavy man-laid rocks and splash onto the concrete slab that warns people not to get any closer. Over the years, people have been dragged into the violent sea when storms erupt. They once were rare, but the weather here is growing more violent as the years pass. Global warming is what people blame.

To me, the sea is freedom; it's a mass of the unknown, so much not discovered. I fill my glass at the sink and continue to watch the relay teams that have crossed the stretch of sea between Ireland and Wales. The groups are large, as no one has ever done it alone. It's dangerous as the rough currents and low temperatures scare away anyone who thinks they are brave enough to try it. Also, the idea that the Irish Sea is home to thirty-five species of sharks makes groups feel far more secure swimming in teams than going it alone.

Today, I'm going to jog along the sea. I'm dressed in a light zip-up sweater, yoga pants, and running shoes. I don't bring music, as I love the sound the sea makes. I always wanted to be the first to row it by myself. Maybe one day.

My father's voice jolts me out of my musing. I empty the remaining water out of my glass into the sink. A kiss is pressed against my cheek before my father speaks cheerfully. "There is my breadwinner; I hope your night went well?"

I cringe internally. What an awkward way to ask me if I got intimate with someone so I could secure my father's business interests. I turn to my father. He's wearing a business suit that fits him perfectly. He's lean for his years and works out most days. "It was interesting," I say before zipping up my sweater fully to give myself something to do other than think about how I was chained or how Diarmuid made me climax.

My God, I didn't want to enjoy it, but it was pure ecstasy. I had tried to fight all the feelings and focus on how he had made me an accessory to murder. Was he serious when he told me that? Did Victor—a priest—give him a command to kill someone? I had so many questions.

"For my sake, spare me the rest of the details. I just hope you do well. We are counting on you." My father pours himself a coffee, and I look at his wide back. No, Ella is counting on me.

My mother wants me to be a ballerina, and my father wants a daughter to give to some sort of cult that promises favors if I'm chosen as a consort. If I fail, I bet that my father's desire for success will weigh more heavily than my mother's dream of a prima donna. A part of me wants to ask my father more about the O'Sullivans, but I know that will raise too many questions, so I keep my mouth shut on the topic.

"I'm going for a run," I say. My father takes a sip of his coffee before assessing what I am wearing.

"You should wear something for the rain; it is expected in an hour or so."

Rain sounds refreshing to me. "I won't be long," I say.

I leave the kitchen and exit the house through the front door that faces away from the sea. The yard has high concrete walls, making our residence private. The yard is small and kept free of plants or anything that would give it color. It's just for cars. A small door to my left brings me out onto the street. To the left will bring me to the sea, and to the right will take me into the small village that has a bus stop. I know what makes me jog right: curiosity and the fact that I might get some answers about the O'Sullivans my own way.

I jog to the small, sheltered bus stop. The local news has been covering the story of a body identified on the outskirts of Rathcoole, a suburb of Dublin. It's the body of Andrew O'Sullivan, uncle of Diarmuid. The obituary states that his funeral is today. So today would be a perfect opportunity to snoop around without fear of running into any of them. I've been curious about where the body of such a high-ranking member of the O'Sullivan family was found. I want to know more about Diarmuid, and this is the only lead I have. I don't want this life, but for my sister's sake, I need to satisfy my parents' hunger so they won't turn to Ella.

No one else is waiting for the bus, and it approaches in the distance. I walk to the edge of the sidewalk as the bus slows down. Using my card tucked in the pocket of my phone case, I purchase a return ticket to Rathcoole. A few people are on the bus, all consumed with their phones. I take a window seat as the bus pulls away, and I have a moment of excitement at going on an adventure. I'd never been brave enough to do this before, but since I was selected as a bride for Diarmuid O'Sullivan, my parents have loosened the leash they normally keep as a chokehold around my neck.

I watch out the window as we pass fields, and before long, the sea opens up and disappears as we enter a more built-up area. I have to switch buses here, and soon, we stop at the small area named Rathcoole. I've never been here before; it's a small village, even enchanting in a way. The buildings are old, and nothing has been updated, but whoever lives here takes great pride in its appearance. All the buildings appear to have a fresh coat of paint on them, each one a different vibrant color, from blues to greens, and I even spot a small pink shop.

The area where I live is suburban; my parents wanted us away from the noise of the city, but the quiet here is almost unsettling. Two people stand at the door of the only supermarket, chatting, and when I jog past, they wave with friendly smiles. It doesn't seem like a place where someone was recently murdered.

I jog to the outskirts of the village. I have no idea of the exact location where the body was found, just that it was here in this sleepy village. I pass a few lone houses, mostly cottages, and I try to see if I can spot garda tape through the sparse undergrowth that grows behind the houses. It grows thicker, and I leave the main road and start my way through the trees and underbrush. A light rain starts to trickle down, and I pause, looking up at the angry sky. The trees rustle around me, birds chirping a song that has me inhaling a lungful of fresh air.

I continue making my way through the tree line. I don't see any tape, and the longer I walk, the heavier the rain becomes. Before long, I'm soaked and thinking of how my father warned me about the change in weather. I should have brought my raincoat. I consider turning back, thinking how foolish this was. What would I find out anyway? Even if I came across the burial site, it wouldn't give me any information. The ground beneath my feet is laced with fallen leaves, and with the recent downpour, it grows slippery. I spin at the sound of a male voice and nearly lose my footing. A hand reaches out and grabs my waist, stopping me from face-planting into the ground.

"Let me go," I say through sheets of rain. The man steps back and raises his hands. "Sorry, I didn't mean to frighten you." He smiles and removes his glasses from his face. Pulling the hem of his sweater, he cleans his glasses before putting them back on. "I'm Rian Morrissey."

His voice is light and happy. Maybe he's a local.

Niamh," I offer up.

"What are you doing out here, Niamh?" he asks, looking around at the trees that surround us. The rain ceases its onslaught, stopping as quickly as it began.

"Looking for something," I say.

His smile widens. "Me, too."

His joyful voice and relaxed stature eased me a bit. He rummages in his pocket and extracts two frube yogurt tubes. He offers me one, but I decline with a shake of my head. I remember having them as a kid, but I haven't in years.

He shrugs and places one back in his pocket before he flips the other around. "Why did the yogurt go to therapy?" he asks, reading the joke off the back.

"I don't know," I answer.

"It had too many cultural issues." He grins and rips the top off before sucking the yogurt from the tube.

"Funny. So, what are you looking for?" I inquire.

He grins. "I could ask you the same thing. But I'm not one for secrets." He glances around us, his brows drawing together. "I'm here to see the burial site of Andrew O'Sullivan." He pushes the empty wrapper into his pocket.

That snippet of information surprises me. "Are you a detective?" I ask. He looks too young to be one.

He continues to smile, but once again, I get a sense that he isn't forcing it; he's just a naturally happy person.

"Kind of. I run a podcast on unsolved crimes."

"How interesting," I say.

He starts to walk, and I fall into step beside him. What kind of luck would it be if he knew something?

"It really is fascinating," he fixes his glasses. "I've loved unsolved crimes ever since James Reyos was proven innocent after spending forty years in prison for a murder he did not commit, thanks to a podcast. I've been trying to achieve the same kind of feat."

"Forty years, really?" I shiver at the thought. Imagine being wrongfully accused and suffering for that long.

Rian nods and smiles. "Yes, forty years of the man's life gone. Poof." He raises both of his hands up, presses his fingers together, then opens them wide. "Just like that. So, I like to keep an eye on unsolved murders. I have a police scanner and fire scanner in my home. It helps me keep up with the emergency calls in the area."

"That's neat," I say, not sure what else to add.

"I arrived at the scene of Andrew's body before the investigators got here. So yeah, it's really neat," he grins again.

"What do you know about Andrew's death?" I probe.

His grin widens. "So, you have an interest in unsolved crimes."

I nod. "Yes," I lie. My interest is only in this crime, in finding out more about Diarmuid, and now Victor is of interest to me.

"You didn't say where you were from." He's suspicious of me now.

"Neither did you," I fire back.

"Touche. Okay, so the scene was discovered by a pair of mushroom pickers. This case is high profile, as the family that Andrew O'Sullivan belongs to has a long-running history of being involved in organized crime."

He glances at me, and I raise my brows as if surprised.

"They say they have left that life, but they all say that. Whatever the O'Sullivans are into now is even bigger and more secretive."

"So, are you a conspiracy theorist also?"

"I don't close off any avenue of investigation. That's what makes me so good."

I want to ask him how many crimes he's solved but resist, as that doesn't really matter here. All I need is information. I don't even have to ask any questions, as he seems happy to offer up all he knows.

"On the day that Andrew was found, he was not the subject of the emergency call. A woman's body was found lying on Andrew's." Rian stops walking, and so do I. "I saw two bodies come out of these woods. I have been trying to see if there are any clues here that the investigators missed. Might have missed on purpose, if my theories are right."

"A woman's body? I never heard about that." Which I hadn't. I want to ask him if he's sure, but he's claiming to have seen it with his own eyes, and if he has a Gardaí scanner that he listened to when the call was made, there is no reason for him to lie to me. But I wonder why no one else knows about the woman's body. Maybe we shouldn't be here; this seems far more dangerous than I thought. Not just one body but two.

"You need to be careful," I say to Rian. He seems nice, and eager to solve this crime, but people like him might get hurt. If someone like Victor knew he was snooping around, would his name end up on some piece of paper in an abandoned post box? Would mine?

"Maybe stick to Gardaí scanners and the internet to do your research."

"What would be the fun in that? Besides, I've already been arrested twice, but I'm determined to find the truth."

The truth. Is it worth the price of someone finding out he has been poking his nose into the burial site? I'm questioning myself for even being here.

I shiver as my damp clothes and hair soaks into my bones. I had forgotten about the rain, too enthralled in what Rian had to say.

"I better go," I say, giving a little wave before turning away.

"You came here for the same reason as I did. You want to know what happened."

The truth is, I don't care what happened; I was seeking some kind of information on Diarmuid and his family, not to find out who murdered a woman.

I don't say anything, and Rian takes a step closer to me. He presses a business card into my hand. "You can call me if you ever want to find out the truth."

I want to hand the card back, but it's Rian who jogs off before I can do so. I glance down at the heavy paper.

When I glance back up, Rian is out of sight, swallowed up by all the trees and underbrush. I pray his curiosity doesn't lead to his ruin.

I stuff the card into my pocket and start back toward the village. I'll dump the card, as I don't want Diarmuid to find out that a man gave me his phone number, not after what happened with the maid. He's far more dangerous than anyone truly knows.

CHAPTER TEN

DIARMUID

Hands of the Kings Edict Five

> *Any member of the order must be committed fully to the order. Personal goals must be cast aside. We live for the order. We live for the betterment of humanity.*

T HE RAIN FALLS IN that persistent, unyielding way that only Irish weather can muster. Standing in the cemetery just outside of Dublin, my men cluster around me, their faces somber, their suits clinging to their bodies as the rain soaks everything. It's a scene straight out of a cliché film, yet here we are, living it in real-time. Only in Ireland would we stand in the rain like this and not think it odd.

The service at St. Gertrude's was a grand affair. Victor's voice, steady and somber, had filled the church, recounting tales of a man whose life had been as complex as the family he left behind. The pews were packed with the O'Sullivan clan and our captains. Among the sea of mourners, I caught glimpses of the Hand of Kings members, their presence a stark reminder of the dual life my family led.

This gathering of secret societies, one hidden within the other, was a testament to the complicated legacy my uncle had woven around us all. And there, amid it all, was Aunt Alicia, her tears flowing with a practiced ease that bordered on theatrical. I knew her grief was expected. Andrew had never shown her kindness, ye, here she was, mourning him as though they'd been close.

Now, as we wait for his final arrival, I can't help but think of my uncle's last demand: a tour of Dublin before his burial.

A final power play from beyond the grave, I think bitterly. He always had to have the last word, even in death, ensuring we'd all be here, drenched and waiting, bound by duty and respect for tradition.

I'm pulled from my thoughts by the approach of one of my men, a newcomer whose name I'm still committing to memory. He rushes over, his apology for lateness nearly lost to the sound of the rain hitting the canopy of umbrellas above us.

"Everything came in just fine, Diarmuid," he says, catching his breath. Rainwater drips from the brim of his hat.

"And who is receiving it tonight?" I ask, shifting my focus to the matters that never seem to pause, not even for death. It reminds me of a poem by W.B. Yeats: in death, he had demanded that all the clocks stop, but time stops for no man.

"O'Boyle's on it," he replies, oblivious to the immediate frown his answer draws from me.

"O'Boyle is on my shitlist," I snap. "Send him for collections. Have Hayes receive instead. We can't afford slip-ups, not now."

"Yes, sir," he responds quickly, turning to relay the instructions.

As he walks away, I turn my gaze back to the cemetery gates, anticipating the arrival of the hearse, my thoughts wandering back to my uncle's life and the intricate web of loyalty, betrayal, and power plays that define it. Even in death, he is still commanding us all. As we stand here, waiting to lay him to rest, I can't help but wonder about the future of the O'Sullivan clan and the secrets we're all bound to keep. Secrets I can't let anyone find out about. My mind reels, thinking that maybe someone in this churchyard knows exactly what I have done.

The rain, relentless in its pursuit, turns the world into a blur of grays and greens by the time Victor arrives. His entrance is, as always, marked by an air of command. He is surrounded by his personal guard, a small group who are loyal to him to a fault and could take out most of us here.

Victor seems to move with deliberate slowness, or maybe it's caution. The ground beneath our feet is slick with rain, glistening like a treacherous carpet under our footfalls. The slope that leads down to the O'Sullivan plot shouldn't be used today, but we have no choice. Andrew has to be laid to rest.

I hope he never rests; I hope the demons are chasing him relentlessly through Hell like he deserves. I watch Victor navigate the slippery descent, and a part of me, dark and unforgiving, wishes to see him falter, to witness him fall and snap his fragile neck, yet the thought is fleeting, chased away by the deeper, more insidious desire that when Victor falls, it will be by my hand and not Mother Nature's.

As Victor passes, the crowd parts, heads bowed in reverence or perhaps fear, whispering "Father" with a mixture of respect and obligation. The title, one he wears as both a mantle and a shield, grates on me. It's a reminder of the power he wields within our family, a power that has shaped our lives in ways both seen and unseen.

The moment is broken by the arrival of the hearse, a sleek, somber vehicle that seems to absorb the light around it. Following close behind is a limo, from which Aunt Alica and Wolf emerge. I step forward, Lorcan and Ronan at my side, to meet them. Aunt Alica's face, usually so composed, betrays a hint of the turmoil beneath, her eyes red-rimmed behind the veil of mourning. Wolf appears stoic, and he offers me a nod of acknowledgment.

As a further insult, Andrew named me as one of his pallbearers. I'm not sure if he knew all along I would take him down, and this was a final slap, or if he truly trusted me enough that he wanted me to carry the weight of his death.

Either way, my men step back as the coffin slides out with ease from the hearse. I'm ready to get this done and over with. I walk to my position, and when we are all ready, I heave the coffin onto my shoulder, and I begin the march toward the grave with the other pallbearers.

Rain drips into my eyes, and it drips off the coffin into the neck of my shirt.

As we make our way down the steep, grass-covered hill, the world seems to tilt beneath my feet. The weight of the casket on my shoulder is too much to bear with the slippery surface beneath. My footing completely slips.

Panic flares within me, hot and immediate. The casket lurches, threatening to escape our grasp and turn this procession into a farce. My legs strain against the sudden imbalance, muscles screaming in protest. In that heart-beat of chaos, a memory crashes through the dam of my consciousness.

I'm back there again, on the cold, unforgiving ground. My uncle's voice, a harsh, grating sound, bellows at me to rise. "GET UP! DAMN YOU, GET UP!" he screams, each word a lash against my already battered body. Pain is my world, a relentless sea in which I'm drowning. The threat of unconsciousness looms, only to be shattered by the cruel cold of a bucket of icy water.

In the shadow of that memory stands Oisin Cormick. He, the hitman whose quiet voice once suggested mercy might be mine. But his words were always lost on my uncle, drowned out by the roar of his own rage. The beatings never ceased, each one a test of my resolve to remain on my feet, to not give in.

But here, on this hill, with the weight of my uncle's casket threatening to drag us all down, something shifts within me. My foot turns sideways. My leg, the one still loyal, pushes against the earth with all the strength borne of years of enduring and overcoming. Muscles I didn't know I could still summon bulge and flex, and miraculously, the casket steadies.

The moment passes in a blur of effort and adrenaline, allowing the other pallbearers to regain their footing. We continue our descent, a bit more wary, but intact. The irony of fighting so hard to prevent the man who taught me about pain from tumbling into disgrace isn't lost on me. As much as part of me would have relished the fall, I can't draw suspicion to myself. Everyone would wonder why I allowed it to happen.

And especially not today, with eyes watching. Always watching.

Someone among the gathered mourners knows the truth of what I did to my uncle.

As we finally reach the bottom of the hill, the cemetery gates loom before us, a threshold between the past and the present. For now, I focus on the steps ahead.

I don't reset until we no longer bear the weight of the coffin and it's lowered into the ground.

As we gather our family and Andrew's friends around the grave, the world seems to hold its breath.

"Diarmuid," Victor's voice cuts through the patter of raindrops, his tone carrying an edge of command that bristles against my already frayed patience.

I turn to face him, schooling my features into a mask of neutrality. "Victor," I reply, my voice steady despite the storm raging within. "A fitting day for a funeral, wouldn't you say?"

His eyes, sharp and calculating, meet mine. "Indeed. The heavens themselves seem to mourn the passing of an O'Sullivan."

I nod, turning away to hide the flash of anger that I know flitters across my face. This is neither the time nor the place for his rub, reminding me that he suspects I am the one who put Andrew in the ground and will one day return for him.

A few more prayers are said over the grave before we all start to leave and find shelter from the harsh rain.

The dim lighting of our usual spot casts shadows across the table where Lorcan, Ronan, and I sit, nursing our drinks in silence. We have all removed our suit jackets and ties. Our shirts are a bit damp, but the heat in the bar will soon warm us up, and the brandies will heat our blood. It's a private corner we sit in at The Church bar, the usual spot we always meet. Today, it is our refuge from the chaos of our lives outside.

Movement close by has us all turning around. Wolf stumbles towards us, his gait uneven, a clear testament to how much he must have drunk already. I glance at Lorcan, and his features tighten. The two women trailing Wolf struggle to match his erratic pace, their expressions a mix of resignation and discomfort.

He opens his arms wide, and a smile that shows his teeth stretches across his face.

"Meet my escorts: $4000 and $3000," he slurs as he gestures to the women.

Lorcan raises an eyebrow, his response dry. "Clever names."

Wolf's grin widens, unfazed by the sarcasm. "I'm being realistic. It doesn't matter what I call them because all I will ever see is what they cost."

Ronan leans forward, his tone laced with disbelief. "I didn't think a man in your line of work would need to pay for prostitutes."

Wolf's laughter is loud, drawing glances from nearby tables; a wave of my hand has them looking away. If they keep looking, I'll have them removed from the premises. "They are not for me, my beautiful cousins. They are yours. My wares. I brought them for you."

"How generous." Lorcan's reply is as sharp as a knife.

Wolf's expression shifts, the drunken facade slipping momentarily to reveal the cold businessman beneath. "I'm not being generous. I am paying you."

Ronan's eyes narrow. "This is a business transaction?"

I remain silent, observing the weight of the moment settling in. Wolf's actions are a grim reminder of the world we inhabit, where everything has a price, and everyone is a commodity. The air between us feels charged, heavy with unspoken questions and the harsh realities of our choices, of my choices. If he knew I took his father's life, what would he do?

"They killed my fucking father!" Wolf's sudden outburst slices through the murmur of the bar like a gunshot, silencing conversations mid-sentence. His pain, raw and unfiltered, hangs heavily in the air, a stark contrast to the drunken haze that had clouded his actions moments before.

Reacting swiftly, I snap my fingers to catch the attention of a nearby waitress. When she approaches, I give her a pointed look and a quick, discreet nod toward the women accompanying Wolf. "Take them to the main part of the bar," I instruct quietly, "and close the door behind you." She nods, understanding, and guides them away with practiced ease, leaving us in a bubble of sudden privacy.

As the door shuts with a soft click, Lorcan guides Wolf to a vacant seat at our table.

"Perhaps she should bring some coffee and water in, yes?" Lorcan suggests eyeing Wolf with a mix of concern and caution.

Wolf's reaction is immediate, a mix of anger and defiance. "Fuck, no! We are drinking tonight."

The weight of the moment is suffocating as I wait to see what Wolf will do. His gaze lands on me, and the drunkenness seems to dissolve. Around us, the bar slowly returns to its usual buzz, the patrons resuming their conversations, their laughter a distant echo against the backdrop.

Wolf finally looks away from me. "I'm drinking; I don't give a fuck what you are doing."

Ronan attempts to intervene. "I don't think there is room in you for more alcohol," he says.

But Wolf is beyond reasoning, his grief morphing into a bitter resolve. "No, no, no. It's never enough. It won't be enough. Not until the son of a bitch that killed my father is dead. Not just dead. Mutilated. Did you hear what they did to him, Ronan? Did you hear?"

I nod, my expression somber. "We heard, Wolf. I'm sorry for your loss," I say, the words slipping out in a tone that suggests empathy. Inside, I'm amused, finding a dark humor in the situation. The irony of apologizing for a deed I did isn't lost on me.

Wolf's reaction is swift, his pain translating into anger. "I don't want to hear another fucking person say that to me. Look, we made a deal, right? With those cult motherfuckers?"

Lorcan glances around nervously. "Wolf, keep your voice down," he hisses, the tension in his voice betraying his concern for our secrecy.

I lean back casually. "The door is closed, Lorcan. This room is soundproof." My reassurance is meant to ease the tension but also to assert control over the situation. Wolf needs to calm down.

Wolf snaps at Lorcan, "Yeah, shut the fuck up, Lorcan." His dismissiveness sparks a snort of amusement from Ronan.

Wolf continues. "We made a deal with those cult motherfuckers that we would do what they say as long as they help us with our shit. Well, we need help. We need every secret asshole they have to get in on this."

I exchange a glance with Lorcan, unable to resist a jab. "Did you hear that, Lorcan? Secret assholes." My words are laced with sarcasm, a light jab in the otherwise tense atmosphere.

Lorcan, unamused, fires back dryly. "I don't play for that team."

Wolf's eyes, burning with a mix of grief and determination, lock onto each of us in turn. "I'm serious, guys. Look, we are family. The four of us in this room. Fuck

Victor. Fuck the Kings. Fuck all of them. We need to take care of our own. Whatever we need to do to get to the guy who did this, we will do it."

Ronan's voice is steady, and his decision is immediate. "I'm in."

Lorcan's shock is palpable. "What?"

Ronan doesn't falter. "I know that you are nervous about your upcoming election, dear brother, but Wolf is right. An O'Sullivan has been maimed and murdered. If we don't make an example of the person who did this, it can happen to any of us. I'll do most of the dirty work, but can you pull some strings if I need it?"

Lorcan, after a moment's hesitation, nods. "Yeah. I can do that."

All eyes turn to me, the final piece of this precarious puzzle. The weight of their stares is a tangible thing, pressing down with the gravity of the situation laid bare before us. Wolf's sex trade, Ronan's legal enterprises, Lorcan's government ties—each plays a critical role in the fabric of our syndicate. But I'm the assassin who will be expected to kill the person who took Andrew's life. Funny how this is all coming full circle, and being part of this circle gives me full control.

"I'm in," I say, my voice steady, betraying none of the turmoil churning within.

As we sit in the dim light of our secluded meeting place, a pact is forged. The waitress arrives at our table with fresh brandy for everyone. I hadn't even noticed anyone ordering the drinks. But Lorcan sits beside the small buzzer that goes directly to the bar. He must have been the one.

He doesn't appear happy but raises his glass. When the door closes, we all do the same. "To justice," he declares.

"To killing the motherfucker who killed my father," Wolf chimes in.

We all click glasses, and I have no idea how I'm going to pull this off.

Chapter Eleven

Selene

The soft glow of the evening light filters across my vanity mirror, casting a warm hue on the array of make-up and hair products scattered in front of me. I'm seated comfortably, the chair's plush cushion a small comfort as I unroll the curlers from my hair, each lock falling into place with a gentle bounce. My reflection stares back at me, a mix of anticipation and nerves for tonight's work event. It's not every day you get to represent your department at such a prestigious gathering.

Just as I secure the last curl into place, a knock at the door has me pausing, glancing at the clock. Who could it be at this hour? I stand, smoothing out my dress before making my way across the main room of my apartment. The hardwood floor feels cool under my bare feet, a sharp contrast to the warmth of the room heated by the late afternoon sun.

Opening the door, I'm greeted by the familiar face of my grandfather, his eyes carrying a mix of apology and concern.

"I'm so sorry, a chroí," he starts, his voice carrying the soft lilt. "I know you are getting ready for your work event, but you have a visitor."

I tilt my head, puzzled. "Who is it?"

He steps aside, revealing a figure. Niamh stands there, her teeth chattering, eyes wide with what appears to be fear or shock, and a tight grip on something in her hand.

"Selene! I need to talk to you!" Her voice is urgent.

I nod to my grandfather, mouthing a silent thank you for bringing Niamh here. "I'll take it from here," I assure him, my voice steady despite the flurry of questions swirling in my mind.

Gently, I place my hands on Niamh's shoulders, guiding her into the warmth of my apartment. The door shuts with a soft click behind us. The contrast between the cozy interior and the crisp air outside makes me aware of the tremble in Niamh's frame.

"What's going on?" I ask, leading her toward the sofa. My heart races, not just from the disruption, but from concern for my friend standing before me, who is visibly distressed.

"I didn't know where else to go, and I know we are not exactly friends, but we could be friends. I mean, in different circumstances—"

"Shush for a moment. We need to get you warm. Take off your clothes," I interrupt her. All I can do is wonder what has happened. And why has she come to me.

Niamh looks around my apartment for the first time and hesitates

"Oh, for Peter's sake. I'll turn around. Take off those clothes, and wrap yourself in the blanket from the couch. Really. How can you possibly still be shy with me?" We have seen each other naked and even heard each other's cries of pleasure.

Niamh's cheeks pinken, but she nods, and I turn around to give her some time to get changed. I hear the wet clothes hit the floor and then it sounds like she settles herself onto the couch.

"Okay," she whispers, her voice still trembling.

She's wrapped herself in the thick blanket, and more color floods her face, but her shivers are still there, still visible in her hands that tighten on the blanket.

I sit down beside her. "Now, how did you find me?" I ask.

"It was an ordeal," she says.

"All right?"

She nods and pauses as if trying to gather her thoughts. "I had my phone, but I don't have it anymore. I mean, oh God, I am so cold."

I want answers but I don't press any further. Instead, I get up and move to the kitchen to put on the kettle. I get down a cup and make her a steaming cup of tea. She accepts it and wraps her cold fingers around the mug.

I wait as she takes a few sips. But there is a wildness in her gaze, as if she's afraid.

"You're safe here, Niamh."

I can't help but feel a twinge of something—pity, perhaps. Her presence here, in my home, is a testament to her desperation.

"I found your parents' address online. Most addresses are online if you've lived in one place for a long while," she confesses, her voice steadier now with the warmth of the tea seeping into her bones.

The mention of my parents sends a jolt through me. "You went to my parents?!" I can't keep the shock from my voice, the thought of Niamh encountering them, of all people.

"And I'm so sorry that I did. I just assumed that you were living at home like Amira and me. I didn't realize that your parents are—"

"—assholes," I finish for her, a bitter laugh escaping me. It's a harsh word but fitting. Their estrangement is a wound that's never fully healed.

"YES. I'm so glad you said it," she agrees, a flicker of a smile gracing her lips.

"My parents gave you this address?" The very idea that they'd help, even slightly, is surprising.

"Yes, but it was a trip getting here. I was jogging, and then I needed to find you. It has been raining for hours. I tripped, and my phone went into a gutter, but I still have this!" Niamh raises her fist, clutching something tightly.

"And what is this?" I ask.

Niamh opens her hand to reveal a business card with a phone number on it.

"A guy's phone number, and I shouldn't have it." She looks down at the card with a frown.

"Okay?" I have no idea where this is going. Does she no longer want to marry Diarmuid? Is this what it's all about?

Niamh releases a long sigh. "I wanted to find out more about Andrew O'Sullivan, Diarmuid's uncle who was murdered."

I nod. "I heard about that."

"So, I went to the village where his body was found."

"I bumped into Rian, a podcaster who likes to look into unsolved murders. He was looking into the case of Andrew O'Sullivan. It wasn't just Andrew's body found at the burial site; they found a woman's, too."

This surprises me; I hadn't heard anything about a second body. "Do you know who the woman is?" I ask.

Niamh shakes her head and takes another sip. "That's why Rian gave me his number. He said if I was interested in what happened, I could ring him."

"Are you going to ring him?" I ask.

Would I ring him? Would I want to know more? I'm not sure.

"I don't know," Niamh answers honestly before sipping her tea.

I checked the time; we don't have much left before the event.

"So, what are you planning to do to get ready for tonight?" I ask, watching her closely. Niamh's reaction is immediate, a mix of confusion and dawning realization.

"What do you mean? What's tonight?" Her voice is tinged with genuine puzzlement, the weight of her earlier ordeals clouding her memory.

I can't suppress a slight smile at her baffled expression. "The annual Diners of Influence event at the Hand of Kings mansion," I remind her, emphasizing the importance of the evening. This event is not just any social gathering; it's a cornerstone of our community's calendar.

Niamh's face drains of color, panic rising in her eyes like a storm surge. The reminder seems to hit her with the force of a physical blow.

Seeing her distress, I step in, a surprising sense of protectiveness washing over me. I've felt protective of her since meeting her; it's nice to take care of someone else and forget my worries for even just a moment. "Don't worry. I've got it," I assure her, my voice gentler than I would have expected. It's a strange sensation. But, I recognize it for what it is: I want a friend.

I lead her to the bedroom, my mind already racing through the logistics of preparing us both for the evening. "Take a shower," I instruct firmly, pointing towards the bathroom.

Niamh nods, still wrapped in the blanket, and enters the bathroom, closing the door after her.

While she's in the shower, I turn my attention to the wardrobe, laying out dresses on the bed. Each piece is beautiful and sexy, designed to make an impression. I've laid out the last dress when Niamh emerges from the bathroom wrapped in a towel, her hair damp and her expression wary. She surveys the dresses I've chosen, a flicker of admiration in her eyes quickly overshadowed by concern. "I'm worried about showing off my shoulders," she admits, her voice small. "My mother always called them manly."

I meet her gaze; all the dresses are sleeveless. "They're not manly; they're strong. Men don't own strength." It's a declaration, a challenge to the insecurities that have been unfairly thrust upon her. It seems I'm not the only one with an asshole for a mother.

As we dress, the room transforms into a whirlwind of fabric, shoes, and accessories. I help Niamh with her jewelry, hair, and makeup, each step bringing us closer to the image of sophistication and power we aim to project.

"Why are you helping me?" Niamh asks, her voice laced with wonder as I apply her makeup with careful strokes.

"I'm not concerned about the results of this competition between us," I reply truthfully. This night, this event, transcends our personal battles. There's something greater at stake, a realization that's slowly dawning on both of us.

Niamh's next question catches me off guard, a piercing look in her eyes. "All of us are here because we have something to lose. What do you have to lose?"

For a moment, I'm speechless, the question striking at the heart of my own fears and doubts. "I have no idea," I confess, the admission more revealing than I intended. It's a moment of raw honesty.

The two of us are now ready for the event, and we both look at ourselves in the full-length mirror.

I still see the shadow of fear in her gaze.

"The woman….from the grave?" I start.

Niamh nods. "I've been thinking about her, too."

I smooth down my navy dress before turning away from the mirror. "She probably has a family out there. Someone waiting for her to come home." I frown; that must be horrible.

"Someone who misses her." Niamh continues as she turns to me.

There is a brief silence between us. It's wrong that no one knows who she is or that she is dead. Why was it kept out of the spotlight? But with Rian's help, we might be able to get answers.

I nod at Niamh, a confirmation of what we should do. "Then, let's get her home."

Niamh smiles. "I agree." Before we leave, she picks up the card with Rian's number on it and stuffs it into the pocket of her dress.

CHAPTER TWELVE

DIARMUID

Hands of the Kings Edict Six

Kings are made to lead our world, but they must be guided. One Hand shall place the Kings in their places. One Hand should make Kings. One Hand should destroy Kings.

T HE RAIN HAS CEASED its relentless assault on the world outside, leaving behind a serene yet sodden landscape. As I step onto the Hand of Kings manse's grounds, the aftermath of the storm is immediately apparent. Every surface, every leaf and blade of grass, is sheathed in a heavy coat of raindrops, like nature's own jewelry. The lights from the manse cast their glow onto the gardens and lawns, turning the water droplets into shimmering diamonds.

I hand my coat to the doorman, but he doesn't make eye contact. In fact, he barely acknowledges my presence beyond the necessities of his role. I suppress a smirk, finding a twisted amusement in their obedience.

The grandeur of the manse never fails to impress, a testament to the power and prestige of its occupants. But tonight, it feels different.

As I step into the warmth of the place, the murmur of conversation and the subtle strains of music greet me. The air is thick with anticipation, every guest playing their part in the night's proceedings. I scan the room, my eyes adjusting to the transition from the dimly lit gardens to the brightly illuminated interior. Here, in this den of influence and intrigue, every smile hides a motive, and every handshake is a calculated move on the grand chessboard.

I navigate through the crowd, acutely aware of the space that seems to open up around me. It's as if my reputation precedes me. I don't mind. Let them whisper, let them speculate.

Good. The last thing I need is drama tonight. As I move through the room, the precise orderliness of everything, from the perfectly pressed uniforms of the staff to the hushed, almost non-existent conversations among the guests, signals Victor's presence.

Michael, Victor's Page, finds me among the throng. His greeting is formal, almost excessively so, but that's to be expected given his position. His is the lowest rank in the Hand of Kings, yet tonight, he bears a message of supposed compassion. "Victor will not be attending the event, but he wanted to extend his condolences," he informs me, his voice steady, betraying no hint of the personal sentiment behind the words—if there even is any.

Victor is rubbing salt in the wound. Finding a chink in my armor. I smile at Michael. "Tell Victor I thank him for his condolences," I say as Michael nods and departs.

As more guests arrive, the dynamic shifts subtly. My brothers, ever predictable, make their customary beeline for the open bar, their nods in my direction serving as our only form of acknowledgment. The crowd is a mix of actors, politicians, religious figures, and even a NASCAR owner/driver. It's a testament to the event's reach and the diverse interests it attracts. The air buzzes with the undercurrent of networking and deal-making.

Then, amid the sea of faces, I spot Niamh and Selene arriving together. Seeing them together shows me they are bonding. I'm not sure how wise that is.

As I watch them make their way through the gathering, the real work of the night begins. Beyond the handshakes, the polite smiles, and the arranged table settings lie the real battleground.

And so, I ready myself to join the fray, my eyes always searching, always assessing. Tonight, like so many nights before, is a game of chess played on a grand scale.

But as I've learned, in this game, every piece has the potential to be a king—or a pawn.

"You ladies look beautiful," I say as Niamh and Selene approach me, two stunning brides. I take each of their hands and place a kiss there that lingers longer than it should. Both blush, and I hope they are thinking about the pleasure I gave them. Both of them were equally delicious.

The moment is shattered when Amira appears. She's barely dressed, her black tight-fitted dress more fitting for risqué entertainment than a high-end gathering. Her lips are painted red, and she reaches up on the tip of her toes and presses her lips to mine. The reaction from the crowd is mixed—a few gasps, a smattering of applause. Amira smiles under the spotlight and gives a shy smile to the crowd.

"Where is the rest of your dress?" Selene's comment is biting, and I suppress a smile at her obvious jealousy. But she is just as stunning as Amira.

Amira grips my hand as if I have chosen her. The thought of pushing up the short black dress and fucking her right here and right now sends waves of pulsing want to my lower regions.

I don't release Amira's hand as the promise in her eyes has my mind reeling.

But the moment is fleeting. Isaac Waryn, the priest with ties to Brien Cahill's departure to the United States, appears at my elbow, pulling me back from the brink of scandalous indulgence.

"Diarmuid, how are you?" he asks, but it's as if he wants to say more. The fact he's even approaching me in the presence of the hand of the kings makes me annoyed. I release Amira's hand.

"Very well, and yourself?" I ask.

"I'm good." He answers and glances around.

"If you can excuse me." I glance at my three brides as my reason not to talk to him.

He seems to understand that this isn't the time or the place. "Could you give me directions to the main dining room?"

I'm ready to tell him where it is when Selene steps forward. "I can show you, Father."

He smiles at her, and she walks away with an eagerness that I think is brought on by her annoyance with Amira's earlier display of affection.

When Selene departs, this leaves Niamh standing alone. She's a vision of elegance and nervous anticipation. She looks incredible, her beauty a stark contrast to the raw, unbridled allure of Amira. And yet, it's Amira who consumes my thoughts, her audacity and the glint in her gaze promising me so much more than …fun, and it ignites a fire within me.

Excusing myself, I take Amira's hand, leading her away from the prying eyes and whispered judgments.

Together, we step out into the night, leaving it all behind. The cool air of the evening envelops us, a welcome respite from the intensity of the manse's interior. In this moment, with Amira by my side, I will be uninterrupted in exploring the depths of desire and defiance that she so effortlessly showcases.

"Where are we going?" Amira asks. I wait for shyness to soak into her gaze but only excitement and want is there.

I have the same want, and I hold out my hand, and she easily slips hers into mine.

"I believe the last time we were together, we got sidetracked," I say, thinking about how the maid had struck her.

She nods. "You took care of it." She stops walking and smiles up at me.

I reach out and cup her face. "You are mine to take care of."

She inhales a quick breath that makes her breast strain against the soft, silken fabric of her flimsy dress.

I lead Amira toward a secluded sanctuary known only to a few. The fountains, now silent and drained for the season, offer a hidden alcove of privacy.

The farthest fountain, hidden from the view of the manse's windows, is where I take Amira. Here, the oversized vases that once adorned the walkway are absent, leaving behind square slabs of marble that serve as pedestals. With care, I remove my hand from Amira's and take off my coat. I spread my jacket over the cold marble, a makeshift bed.

Amira bites her lip as she glances down at the jacket, and as if sensing my intentions, she lies down and spreads her legs. The dress rides up higher, revealing tanned thighs.

The cold is forgotten as we both yearn for the same thing. I kneel between her legs, and her gaze remains transfixed on me. Like she doesn't want to miss a moment. Dipping my hand and sliding it up her thigh and slipping one finger under the black panties she wears, I don't stop until the warm folds give me access, and she moans loudly. I move my finger in and out before pushing in two fingers; when I remove them, I place my fingers in my mouth. I want to take my time with her, but our disappearance will not go unnoticed.

She spreads her legs further, the dress now riding at her midriff as I unbuckle my belt and push my trousers and boxers down far enough to release my raging cock. I need this release so badly, and Amira seems to be the only one willing. I will have all three, but tonight, it will be Amira.

The minute I bend down to place my cock at Amira's opening, her hands find my shoulders, and she's pulling me to her with a greed I can easily match. The minute I slide my cock in, her folds stretch around me, and I lower myself. Her fingers curl around my shoulders; her eyes widen at the sudden intrusion between her legs.

I can't be gentle or slow, and I'm not. Amira lies still under me, her eyes tightly shut as I start to push my full length into her. Her teeth clamp down on her lip as if she is stopping herself from screaming out. I don't want her to scream and draw attention to us. I pound faster and harder; her eyes snap open, and before she can make a sound, I press my lips to hers and grip her hips, demanding her body to open up further for me.

I don't stop until I'm fully in, and then I fuck her like I want to. She cries into my mouth, and it's delicious as I take her virginity under the fountain. The faster I go, her cries turn to whimpers before they morph into moans that have her opening her eyes and looking into mine. With our mouths barely touching each other's, we breathe and pant as I fuck her until I release my seed into her body. She cries out only seconds later, her own release washing over my cock that's still wrapped in her warm folds. The muscles tighten and clench around me like they are demanding every last drop of my cum, and I'm happy to oblige.

Afterward, we make our way to the main dining room. We arrive just before Victor, the man whose presence dictates the rhythm of the night. His voice is a familiar drone that I scarcely register. My focus is elsewhere, lost between Amira and Michael's earlier words that Victor wasn't coming. Was that message only for me? What was Victor playing at?

As we walk, I glance at Amira. On our way back, rain has started to fall, and one raindrop traces a slow, deliberate path between Amira's breasts. It's a distraction until we are ushered to our table.

Niamh, one of my brides, has her attention fixed on her plate, a deliberate attempt to remain unseen, unnoticed. Selene, however, offers a stark contrast. She isn't eating, her plate untouched, her focus not on the food but on me. Her eyes hold a tempest, fury, and accusation woven together in a silent rebuke that speaks louder than words ever could.

She's furious.

Chapter Thirteen

Selene

As I guide Isaac Waryn toward the main dining room, a sense of guilt tugs at the corners of my heart. I couldn't help but feel a pang of regret for leaving Niamh behind. It was never my intention. In my mind, I assumed she would know she was welcome to join us. It seems I assumed too much.

Next time, I need to just tell her to come. The last thing I want is to create distance between us over a misunderstanding. I would hate for Niamh to think I had intentionally left her with Amira.

Walking beside the priest, a habit from countless similar events, prompts me to almost offer him my arm. But the memory of his clerical collar stops me mid-gesture. Sure enough, Father Waryn continues with his hands clasped behind his back, maintaining a respectful distance. I smile at a few people who are curiously looking our way. I know my dress is very fitting here. The rich blue ballgown is the exact same color as my eyes.

"I'd imagine that you feel embarrassed about what we just witnessed back there," Isaac says while looking over the crowd also, and nodding at people whom I have no idea who they are.

He's referring to the earlier incident—an uncomfortable moment that I wish could be erased from memory. "You imagine correctly," I admit, the words heavy with apology. "I'm so sorry for her behavior, Father. She wasn't raised right."

Isaac glances at me. "I may be a man of the cloth, but I wasn't born in a monastery. New love is a strong emotion that can make us do all sorts of foolish things."

His words catch me off guard, sparking a defensive reflex. "I beg your pardon, Father, but they are not in love." My tone is sharper than intended, a reaction to the assumption that doesn't fit the reality. Amira is cruel and trying to grab attention. None of us know Diarmuid, so whatever any of us are feeling, it isn't love.

Isaac's next question halts me in my tracks. "Then, if I may ask, what is the situation between you?"

"Father?" My voice betrays a flicker of confusion, mingled with apprehension.

Taking a moment, I let my gaze wander through the ornate hallway, appreciating the brief bit of privacy before we reach the bustling main dining room. The silence here is a stark contrast to the lively chatter that awaits us, and yet, my heart races with a nervous energy.

The thought of engaging in conversation with a priest, above all people, makes me want to run.

"I'm afraid I don't understand your question, Father," I finally say, attempting to mask my discomfort with confusion. Isaac's gaze meets mine.

"Or you are afraid to answer it," he counters gently.

"Maybe," I concede, the word barely a whisper. Admitting even this much feels like standing on the edge of a precipice, unsure of the fall.

Isaac's tone softens. "Whatever your relationship with that man, please let me give you a warning." It's not his tone or his body language that sends off all the alarm bells in my body; it's his gaze. He's afraid.

"He has a job. This job is important for his employers. It is a job that no one else can do quite as well or as…eagerly." His choice of words sends a chill down my spine, bringing to mind the O'Sullivan mafia ties.

My mind races, trying to piece together Isaac's cryptic message. Before I can form a response, he continues, "There are bad people in this world, my child. The worst kind performs the worst sins imaginable, and they do it for pay. You see, there was this child—"

His revelation is abruptly cut off by the sound of footsteps. Someone emerges from the dining room, passing us with a glance before disappearing down the corridor.

"A child?" I'm clasping the priest's arm.

He appears uncomfortable all of a sudden. "I've said too much." The priest glances into the bustling dining room.

"You've said nothing." I want to know what he is saying. "Did Diarmuid hurt a child?" Revulsion tightens my core.

The priest shakes his head, but something doesn't feel right. "But he hurts people?" I prod quietly.

The priest doesn't answer, but he doesn't have to. I see it in his gaze.

Oh god. My mind trips and races over his earlier words. *"He has a job; this job is important to his employers."* If he's part of the mafia and hurts people, does that make him a hitman?

The realization crashes into me with the force of thunder: Diarmuid is a hitman. My mind races, trying to reconcile the man I thought I knew with the stark reality Isaac's words have painted.

As we approach the grand doors of the main dining room, Isaac's gesture for silence—fingers pressed to his lips—halts any questions I might have had. The bustling energy of the room engulfs us. I find my seat beside Niamh, scanning the room for familiar faces. The absence of Amira and Diarmuid doesn't surprise me.

"Where are they?" I whisper to Niamh, trying to sound casual.

"Diarmuid led Amira outside," she replies, her tone indifferent.

I lean closer to Niamh, my voice low but urgent. "Don't go off alone with Diarmuid. Stay beside me for the rest of the night, all right?" The protective instinct in me flares to life, a fierce need to protect her from the man we are both promised to.

I watch as Diarmuid and Amira enter the dining hall. Both of them are a bit disheveled looking. Disgust makes my stomach turn.

He deserves Amira. I can't bring myself to eat, my appetite stolen by the revelation of Diarmuid's true nature. My gaze fixates on him, a silent accusation. Disgust bubbles within me.

A part of me knows I should act pleasant; after all, I was groomed for him. My parents' warnings echo in my mind, foretelling dire consequences if I fail to secure my place by his side. Yet, at this moment, their threats feel distant.

My resolve hardens, a defiant flame burning away any lingering doubts. I refuse to bind my fate to a killer's.

After pushing my food around my plate and listening to distant babble and Amira's loud giggles, I excuse myself from the table.

"I need to use the ladies' room," I say as I stand. I don't look at Diarmuid or Amira but focus on Niamh. She rises straight away. "Me, too."

Niamh follows me upstairs, where there are no guests. I know there is a bathroom up here that we used before when we were requested to go to gatherings with Diarmuid.

It's our little haven, a brief respite from the calculated smiles and watchful eyes. As we close the door behind us, the clamor of the party below fades to a distant murmur, and I take a deep breath, bracing myself for the conversation ahead.

"I found out something about Diarmuid," I begin, my voice steadier than I feel. The weight of the secret presses against my chest. "He's a hitman." Saying it out loud causes my stomach to tighten.

Niamh's reaction is immediate. She covers her mouth with her hand and turns away. "The day he took me to church, he stopped at a post box and had me get an envelope out of it. When I gave it to him, he said it was from Victor, and the name on it was the person he was commanded to kill."

Oh God. Revulsion pours through me, but along with it comes fear. *It's true.* He's a hitman and for Victor.

"What are we going to do?" she asks, her voice tinged with a vulnerability I've rarely heard from her. The question hangs in the air. I have no idea. It's not like we can walk away from Diarmuid.

"Is that why you were digging into Andrew's death?" It made such sense. Niamh didn't seem like the snooping type. Her shaken state when she arrived at my apartment, her desperation to find out more was now adding up.

Before she can answer me, the door swings open. Amira saunters in, her laughter cutting through the tension like a knife. "Oh, shoot. I thought that I would be the only one up here," she says, a smirk playing on her lips.

"Coming up to pick the grass blades out of your ass?" I retort, unable to keep the bitterness from my voice. It's a petty jab, but I'm not in the mood for her games.

"Oh wow, slut shaming, are we?" Amira fires back, her tone mocking. It's clear she's not the least bit bothered by my comment.

"I don't care about you having an active sex life, but don't you think we should be making a good impression at an event like this?" I counter.

"Check the dew on the marble outside. My ass made a great impression," she quips, unfazed.

"Whatever. You can have him, Amira. We would much rather just be dropped so we can go on with our lives," I say finally.

As Amira laughs off my words, I turn to Niamh, seeing my own resolve reflected in her eyes.

Amira's laughter fills the space between the sterile walls of the bathroom, her amusement making me tighten my fists. "You really are morons," she says, her voice laced with disdain.

"You don't understand…" Niamh says, her face is unnaturally pale even under the makeup I had applied not long ago.

Amira cuts her off. "I understand. What? Do you think that if Diarmuid rejects you, you just get to go on with your merry lives?"

"Well, I know that I would have to figure out a Plan B, but basically, yeah," Niamh says.

"Why couldn't we?" I challenge.

Amira's response is a mix of arrogance and pity. "Oh my God, I should just let you go. I would win him, and you guys can figure it out yourselves. Luckily for you, I am already winning, so I don't mind being nice." Her words drip with condescension. I want to tell Niamh to forget it. We don't need to listen to Amira's words. She's just on a high from having Diarmuid.

"Once you become a Bride, you belong to them. Even if you get rejected, you still belong to them. Understand?" Amira's tone shifts, the gravity of her statement hanging heavily in the air.

Niamh's confusion mirrors my own. "What do you mean?" she asks, her voice small.

The implications of Amira's words are chilling. The idea of being forever bound, with no true escape, is a cage I hadn't envisioned. I had naively assumed that rejection would be a release, a chance to reclaim my life and start anew. I knew I'd have to face my parents' wrath, but never being free of this world sends a cold dread that settles in my stomach.

This is a fate I can't accept. My mind races, desperate for a solution, a way out.

As Amira stands before us, a smirk playing on her lips, I realize that our understanding of the situation has been naïve at best. How does Amira know all this, and we don't?

Amira's words cut through the air, each one landing with the weight of a verdict. "Diarmuid is a Duke, right? He is supposed to become a King?"

"In the mafia?" Niamh asks, before glancing at me.

Amira's laugh is humorless, sharp. "No, dumbass. In the Hand of Kings. You really have no idea what you have gotten yourself into. They are like the Illuminati, but they never fell. Hundreds of years of building power, and you are a Bride of a future King. If you fail, no other King or Duke is going to want you, so you get passed to the Marquesses, then the Earls, and so on. Fail enough times, and Wolf will get you."

"Who's Wolf?" The question escapes my lips before I can stop it, a reflection of my growing horror. Each word that leaves Amira's mouth keeps getting worse and worse.

Amira's answer sends a shiver down my spine. "Diarmuid's cousin. He operates the O'Sullivan sex trade."

The room spins as the gravity of our situation becomes painfully clear. Niamh and I exchange a look of shock, our shared fear unspoken but palpable. The world we thought we knew, the dangers we believed we understood, pale in comparison to the nightmare Amira unveils.

She has got to be lying. But why would she?

"You can try to run, but you won't get far. Your passport will magically stop working. Your family will be stalked. Your money will disappear." Amira's voice is cold, matter-of-fact.

"Face it, ladies. Your options are on Diarmuid's arm or someone's whore." The finality in Amira's statement is a death knell. She doesn't seem to care how we are taking this as she turns to the mirror and fixes her hair. She smiles at herself.

Panic wells up within me, a tide of desperation and fear threatening to drown my resolve. The thought of being passed down the hierarchy of power like a pawn in a sick game is unbearable. And Wolf... the mere mention of his name and his vile trade sends a wave of nausea crashing over me.

Beside me, Niamh's eyes are wide with the realization of what Amira is saying. The revelation of the Hand of Kings, of the real power and darkness behind Diarmuid's position, casts a shadow over any hope of escape.

It can't be like this. Amira spins and gives us one final look. "Best of luck." She leaves the bathroom, and I can't seem to find my footing.

Something ignites in me, a spark of defiance. The fear is overwhelming, yes, but the thought of succumbing without a fight is intolerable. I glance at Niamh, seeing my own determination mirrored in her eyes. No matter how dire the situation, we can't let fear dictate our fate.

"We'll find a way," I whisper, more to myself than to her. "We have to." With every fiber of my being, I vow to fight, to seek a sliver of hope in this darkness—for Niamh, for myself, for our very souls.

CHAPTER FOURTEEN
DIARMUID

THE CHANDELIERS CAST A warm, luxurious glow over the long dining table. I sit, somewhat stiffly, in my designated seat of honor, surrounded by the echoing laughter and the clinking of fine china. This dinner is Victor's doing, a chance to parade the prestige of our order before eyes hungry for the slightest hint of weakness. But to me, it feels like a gilded cage, each course a rib in the frame.

The starter arrives, a tiny marvel in the bowl of a spoon, crafted by a French chef whose name escaped me as quickly as he had introduced himself.

Next, the scallops, a sea-kissed treasure from the cold waters of Bedford, Massachusetts, are placed before us. They're seared to perfection, a testament to the journey they've undergone to grace our plates. Yet, as the flavors unfold on my tongue, I can't help but crave something as simple as a pot of stew.

The main course is presented with a piece of A5 Wagyu beef so small it almost seems lost on the expansive porcelain. The chef from Kobe, who had tenderly prepared it, speaks of the beef as if it were a piece of fine art.

As the courses parade before us, each more elaborate than the last, my thoughts drift to the real reason behind this grand display. I've watched other Dukes undergo this bridal ritual, a test to see how potential Consorts fit in with high society.

Amira shifts her chair subtly yet decidedly closer to mine, her movement smooth and deliberate. She has drawn the attention of nearly everyone in the room. It isn't hard to see why. Her dress, if one could call it that, openly displays her cleavage. The small black spaghetti straps are tiny on her tanned shoulders, and I know when she stands, the dress will barely cover her. The fabric clings to her form in a way that leaves little to the imagination. Plunging necklines and daring slits were its signature, making it a piece more suited for a sultry night out than a fine dining experience. The smirk on her face and joy in her eyes suggested she was fully aware of the effect she had, reveling in the attention. As much as I tried to focus on the culinary artistry before us, I can't ignore how sexy she is.

"Are you enjoying the meal?" She coos up at me, her hand slowly moving under the table to rest on my leg. I thought after having her, my need would die down, but now it starts to grow again.

"It's delicious," I declare.

Even though I want her body, I can't help but feel a sense of distrust with Amira. She is someone who seems to crave the spotlight with such intensity. Was it a result of neglect, a plea for attention unmet by her parental figures, or simply a facet of her personality?

I glance at Niamh. She barely makes a ripple in the social currents of the dinner. Her modesty and poise suggest years of discipline. In her is a quiet strength, a resolute spirit that doesn't need the limelight to affirm its worth. Maybe she would be better suited to me.

I shift my leg away from Amira's touch, and straightaway, a frown appears on her face.

My gaze then drifts to Selene. She elegantly navigates the raspberry champagne sorbet. She must sense me watching her as her gaze clashes with mine. In that glance, I see not just her earlier anger or irritation but a challenge, an invitation to delve deeper than the surface. It's an anger that isn't raw or uncontrolled but calculated, a reflection of a mind as sharp as it is beautiful.

She drops her gaze from mine, not in shyness, but as if she has seen enough.

So, have I had enough? As the last course is served, people retire to the lounge. The ladies leave to refresh themselves, but not before I notice one last look from Selene. She intrigues me.

The lounge I enter is quiet. I select a glass of whiskey from a tray of assorted spirits.

I take my drink and step out onto the balcony, where I'm greeted by the cool evening air, a stark contrast to the heated atmosphere of the dining hall. The whiskey burns a path of warmth as I sip, watching the driveway stretch out before the main door.

Lorcan's presence is announced not by the sound of his footsteps but by the shared understanding of needing a moment away from the festivities. He leans against the balcony railing beside me, his gaze fixed on the darkness beyond.

"Twelve courses." He finally breaks the silence, his voice carrying a mix of awe and incredulity.

"Yes," I reply.

"Twelve fucking courses," he repeats, with a chuckle that borders on disbelief.

I lift my drink in a silent toast to his observation. "I'm having my thirteenth now," I say, a smile tugging at the corner of my mouth.

Lorcan laughs.

"I noticed that you had an extra appetizer," Lorcan says, his voice casual, as if he's commenting on the weather.

"I won't talk about this," I respond firmly. What I do with my Brides is private, and my business alone.
"Come on, you know that Ronan or I will be next. I just want a little bit of information," Lorcan persists, but his 'just' feels heavier than it sounds.

"My moments with them are mine," I say again.

I can almost sense Wolf approaching before he steps out onto the balcony and joins me and Lorcan. His steps are heavy. He's already been drinking, a fact that surprises none of us. It's become part of his persona, a shield as much as a weakness.

"I need a gun," he slurs slightly.

"Wolf, this is not the place," I respond instantly.

His words become reckless, teetering on the edge of madness. "Well, if anyone tells the authorities, I'll just kill them. People are allowed to do that in Ireland. No one gets punished if you kill someone in Ireland," he proclaims, a twisted smile playing on his lips, oblivious to the gravity of his own words.

Lorcan's response is immediate, his voice laced with anger and fear. "Shut the fuck up, man. Get a hold of yourself! The fucking cardinal is over there." His eyes dart towards the dignitary, a silent plea for Wolf to recognize the danger of his rantings.

Wolf, however, seems lost in his own vendetta, his voice rising. "Perfect. I can ask his forgiveness after I kill my father's murderer."

It's then that Ronan appears, his question simple yet loaded with concern. "What the hell is going on here?"

"Wolf is trying to drag our entire business down," I explain.

Ronan nods, understanding flashing in his eyes. "We need to get him away from everyone before someone tells Victor."

Together, we box around Wolf and try to guide him back to the house. But he's being awkward, pushing against us. I shove him; he wobbles but rights himself. The guests' curious gazes feel like spotlights on us, but a glare from me is enough to make them avert their eyes, a silent command they dare not disobey.

As I help Wolf up the stairs, I hear the front door open. Looking down, I catch a glimpse of Niamh exiting, her silhouette graceful and determined, with Selene following close behind her.

Their departure is a silent alarm. Selene's exit, with Niamh in tow, is not just an escape; it's a statement, they have bonded. I don't have time to follow them, not with Wolf in such a volatile state.

I focus back on the task at hand, guiding Wolf away from prying eyes and ears before he says something that will get him killed.

But Wolf notices my two Brides leaving too. His finger, unsteady yet determined, points directly at Selene, his words slurred but clear: "Get out while you can, love."

She nods, a silent acknowledgment of a warning perhaps long expected, and leaves without a word.

Wolf's attention, however, swiftly shifts. His gaze moves, heavy with alcohol, and he points upwards. "But you, you can stay." His words float up to Amira, who leans over the railing, curiosity etched into her features.

Anger crashes through me, and in a moment of decision, my hands release their grip on Wolf, a calculated risk. His body, unprepared for the sudden absence of support, sways and then crashes against the banister, the impact sharp and sudden. The combination of the blow and the alcohol coursing through his veins proves too much, and his lights go out, his body slumping to the ground in a heap of silence.

"Alcohol thins the blood, Diarmuid. A hit like that could kill him." Lorcan glances around to see if anyone saw, his disapproval of my actions evident in his tone.

I don't give a fuck. He deserved it.

"Then, half of all our problems are fucking solved," I retort.

Loran and Ronan pick up Wolf and carry him upstairs to a guest room, the effort obviously draining with each step my brothers take. Wolf isn't small by any means.

But I enjoy the view of him slumped over, his feet trailing along the wooden floor. At least he's quiet.

I'm aware that Amira follows closely behind.

"Can you open the door?" Lorcan asks me, glancing over his shoulder. I don't move, so Amira does as my brother asks.

"Thank you, Amira," he says as he and Ronan get Wolf into the room.

Wolf groans loudly from the bed. Amira steps in again. "I'll get a washcloth," she says and disappears into the adjoining bathroom.

The tension in the room thickens as my brothers glance at me. "She is not taking care of him."

"I barely take care of myself; I'm not about to do it for him." Ronan's retort is quick, laced with his own brand of humor and resignation.

"Diarmuid, what is the point of having spare women if you can't get them to mop up a drunk?" It's Lorcan's comment, though, that breaks the strained peace, his words cutting deeper than he probably intends.

The disrespect in his tone ignites something within me. Without fully processing the decision, I find myself pinning Lorcan against the wall, my anger finding a physical outlet. The threat in my eyes is as clear as the words unspoken between us.

Ronan steps in before things escalate further. "There is no need for that," he says, pushing us apart.

Amira returns, her arrival marked by the practical items in her hands—a washcloth, a water pitcher, and a glass. Her posture, one hip jutted out, an eyebrow lifted, speaks volumes, her words cutting through the tense silence. "Either you three have become really close and cuddly, or I missed a fight."

Her comment, light yet pointed, draws no response from us. She moves to the side table, setting down her washcloth and pitcher.

She places the cloth on Wolf's forehead, and he groans again. When none of us move, Amira glances at me. "I can watch over him until he wakes."

"No," I say immediately.

"She's right. Let her watch over him so we can return before people start to notice," Ronan says. If it was Lorcan after his smart-ass comment about Amira, I would be saying no again, but I glance at Amira, who nods at me.

"Go," she says.

With a final nod, we file out of the room. The re-minder of Selene and Niamh leaving has me walking down the stairs.

"Come, we can have a drink," Lorcan calls from be-hind me.

"I have somewhere I need to be," I tell him, my mind already steps ahead of my body.

I find myself outside of Selene's house. The knowledge of where each of my Brides lives is something I found out before they even met me. Selene's home, a convert-ed garage beside her grandparents' house, stands quiet under the night sky.

Knocking on her door, I'm met not with the warm welcome one might hope for but with annoyance. Her expression is clear; her willingness to entertain me, markedly less so.

"May I come in?" I ask as she folds her arms across her chest. Her dress from earlier has been swapped for denim jeans and a loose-fitting sweater.

"No." Selene barks.

I raise my brow. "You know you can't stop me from coming in." I remind her of my power here.

"If I can't stop you from doing whatever you want, then don't fucking ask. Selene fires back, her voice sharp enough to stir the quiet of the night, catching the attention of a neighbor. A light flashes in the dark, and I take another step toward her, but she doesn't back away from the door.

It's clear she doesn't want me in her home, but I'm not giving up. "Let's take a drive, then." I offer an olive branch.

Her expression morphs, showing her discomfort at the thought of being alone with me.

I grit my teeth, not one to bow to the whim of a woman. But I want to know what has made Selene so upset.

"A brief walk down the street. A public place."

She unfolds her arms and lets out a heavy huff. "Fine, wait here." She closes the door in my face. She doesn't keep me waiting for long before she appears with a heavy pair of brown outdoor boots and a heavy cream jacket thrown over her sweater.

"I see you and Niamh have bonded," I start.

"She's very nice." Selene weighs each word.

"And Amira?" I ask.

Selene glances at me now, her gaze intelligent and yet concealed. "You seem to like her."

I hide a smile. Is that jealousy I detect? "I like all three of you."

"Why are you here?" she asks. From meeting her the first three times, my impression of her was that she was always controlled—but not tonight. I wonder what transpired. But I had pegged her as the troublemaker.

"To find out why two of my Brides left so abruptly."

Selene starts walking again. "The night was almost over, and I was tired. So, you came all this way to find out why I left?"

I came for more than one reason. I wanted to get away from Wolf and my brothers' disapproving looks.

I nod.

"I'm not a dumb, spoiled, rich girl. I'm educated. I can tell when people are lying, and you do nothing but lie," she accuses, her voice a mixture of anger and disappointment. Her abrupt words make me stop walking this time.

"I have to be deceitful in my business," I answer honestly. We have so many secrets to carry. Sometimes, the lies can get tangled with the truth.

What business?" she probes, but her voice isn't as sharp anymore.

"Imports," I answer.

"Liar."

"Be careful, sweet Selene," I whisper and give her a warning glance.

"I know what you are." Her voice is heavy, too heavy, and I don't like it.

I immediately go with humor. "Fuck, are you going to call me a vampire?" My attempt to deflect with humor sounds feeble even to my own ears.

"How do you know about that movie?" She counters, a smirk playing at the edge of her words.

"How does an intellectual such as yourself know about that movie?" I retort.

"You are redirecting the conversation," she accuses, pinpointing my tactic with ease before tightening her jacket around her perfect frame.

"You are easy to redirect," I shoot back before I run my thumb along my lips, lips that she glances at for a moment. I swear her blue eyes soften before they ignite again with something close to fear.

"You are a killer," she states, a declaration so raw that it strikes a chord inside me that hasn't been pulled since I was a kid.

"Am I now?" I reply, with a raised brow, attempting to regain control of the conversation, and steering us back into a more humorous footing.

"Stop it! I know what you've done. And who you've done it to," she insists, her voice a mix of anger, fear, and a daring kind of courage.

"You have entered a dangerous world, Selene," I warn.

"So, you've done it. You've killed people. Men, women, and children," she states, a cold summation of my sins laid out in the open, each word a weight, each accusation a mirror reflecting a version of myself I've fought to keep hidden, not just from the world, but from myself.

The discipline of masking my emotions has been a cornerstone of my existence since childhood, a necessary armor forged from the unforgiving punishments from Victor and Andrew. I have perfected the steady stare and a firm lip that has seen me through countless situations. Yet, Selene's accusation causes me to pause. It's a microsecond of hesitation. To any onlooker, it would have been invisible, insignificant. But Selene's eyes widen.

Her reaction is immediate; her breath falters, and then she sprints back toward the safety of her home. Her steps are panicked, and it takes me a moment to respond.

I chase after her. As I run, my mind races, trying to piece together the hows and whys of her accusation. She's made it clear she knows about the killings, the lives I've taken, even mentioning children—a detail so specific, so damning, that it sends a chill through me.

How could Selene know? Her inference, her mention of children, implies she believes Brien Cahill is among my victims.

I push my body harder, and the need to understand and clarify become my sole focus.

She's made it nearly to her home, running alongside the building, when my arm circles her waist, and she's airborne before I swing her and pin her to the wall. She's breathing heavily and, straightaway, she starts to fight me.

As I cover her mouth with one of my hands, anger races through me. "The world isn't fair. Sometimes your parents are shitty, and you have a shitty life. Sometimes, people die who shouldn't have died. Sometimes, a father drives up a gambling debt, so his son gets killed for it." My emotions become erratic; I've never lost control like this, and it isn't fair, but I'm not working to make the world fair. I am working to get what is mine.

Tears fall from her eyes and soak my hand. She stops fighting me, and I remove my hand from her mouth. She licks her tears before she glares at me. "You are a monster."

Her response cuts deeper than any knife I've ever wielded. I agree with her.

I press my body against hers. "I am a monster with clearances, allowances, and ultimate freedom. I could tear into you right now, and nothing would happen to me."

My anger turns to something darker as I look down at her wet lips. Raising a hand, I run my thumb along her bottom lip. She swivels her head quickly away from me. Like my touch disgusts her, I grip her face, forcing her to look at me. "This kind of monster needs to be pleased, or no one is safe."

Her heavy breath fans across my face. My movements are abrupt and almost frantic as I press my lips to hers. She doesn't kiss me back, but that doesn't hinder me from taking what I want.

My tongue shoots out and runs across her lips, forcing them to part. When my hand trails across her breasts and in between her legs, she speaks.

"Please don't." Her plea is soft.

But the darkness she has ignited in me doesn't allow me to stop. "Are you going to stop me?" I ask.

Her gaze darts around the space. "Physically, I can't." She grits her teeth.

"Did you not swear obedience when you became one of my Brides?" I dip my head in and kiss her again before trailing kisses up to her earlobe. "Who told you that I was a hitman?"

When I look back in her eyes, I see her resolve as strong as before. I hate that she is protecting someone.

"Tell me, and I'll stop."

"If I tell you, will you kill the person?" She questions. I grin. "Most likely."

"Then I won't tell you." I hate the thought that she could care for someone else. She must know she's mine; if she doesn't, I will show her.

I run my hand back between her legs, and she tightens her thighs together as if she could stop me.

"You like my touch; I remember how wet you were for me." I pop the first button of her jeans and then pull down the zipper while holding her hands above her head.

"Let's see if you are as repulsed as you are acting?" I dip my finger inside her, and she's wet. I grin in victory.

She tries to wiggle, but my tight hold on her keeps her back firmly against the wall.

"I think my troublemaker likes this," I whisper in her ear again before I push my finger deeper.

"So tell me, who you were talking to?" I insert a second finger, and she gasps, her core tightening around me. She's fucking perfect. As I watch her gaze transform from hate to pleasure, I almost don't want her to tell me who told her. I want to make her come right here and now on my fingers.

I use my thumb to rub her clit as I continue to fuck her with my fingers. I want nothing more than to bend her over and take what is mine, but I'll wait for the right moment for that. For now, she will learn who her master is.

"Give me a name, and I'll stop," I whisper, moving my fingers harder and faster inside her while my thumb circles her clit. She's shuddering, her gaze glazed over.

"No," she whispers as her eyes flutter closed.

I love that she won't give in; I love what I'm doing to her.

She groans, and her core tightens. I work harder on her clit, knowing she's close to coming, and when moisture fills my palm, dripping down from my fingers, I know I have gotten what I wanted.

She comes hard on my hand, and when her body stops shaking, I extract my fingers and lick each one slowly. Her mouth is open as she watches me. "I can keep coming back and doing this until you tell me."

A spark of something flashes in her eye. Maybe she wants me to come back every night.

Tears still stain her face, and she wipes her cheeks with the back of her hand.

Looking at her and into her eyes is a declaration that I am indeed a monster, and she has no intention of telling me.

Chapter Fifteen

Amira

I didn't want Diarmuid to go. I would have liked to spend more time with him. But I'm trying to show him my range—how I can play whatever part he needs—a role that changes between lover and now caretaker of his family's troublesome relatives. Babysitting Wolf will show Diarmuid that I can be a good wife.

Wolf is still asleep as I sit on the side of the bed and examine his face. I can't help but notice the unmistakable family resemblance—the sharpness of his jawbone and the distinctive shape of his brow. They are the same features that Diarmuid and his brothers have. All are extremely handsome.

The light catches the hair on Wolf's cheeks and head, revealing a surprising red tint. A ginger, I muse.

Every so often, Wolf stirs, each time awakening with a parched throat and a confused look in his eyes. He reaches out for a glass of water, his hand shaking slightly.

To him, I'm a stranger—a face without a name. And why should he recognize me? My interactions with Wolf have been fleeting, and the more I've learned about him, the more I've felt a creeping sense of unease.

He is just as deadly as his cousins, maybe more so because Wolf is unpredictable, based on the rumors I've heard. The most disturbing whispers, the ones that send shivers down my spine, are his involvement in the family's sex trafficking ring. I had shared this knowledge with Niamh and Selene with a smile, but inside, my stomach soured.

He starts to cough again, and I sit and watch him struggle to catch his breath. I've heard of people choking on their own vomit. If he does throw up, I won't be able to clean it. Knowing that I need to impress Diarmuid, I rise and walk around the bed, picking up the glass and bringing it to Wolf's lips.

"You're okay; just take a sip." I try out a smile as his gaze focuses on me. He does as I command. The water seems to lodge itself in his throat, and he's sputtering again. A memory thick and hard slices through my mind.

My mother bent over a small bucket as she gasped for air, but there was no forgiveness for all the alcohol she had indulged in. Her hand had reached out to me for help, and I remember standing in the hallway watching her, hoping her last breath would be stolen on the kitchen floor.

Unfortunately, it wasn't.

Wolf gasps and takes in a few lungfuls of air. His brows furrow. He won't remember this tomorrow, so I have nothing to fear. But just in case, I offer words of encouragement. "There you go. You are doing great." The pitcher on the bedside table is empty, and I pick it up and leave to refill it. I'm contemplating using the tap water in the bathroom, but even as a child, I was scolded if I drank from the bathroom taps. The system in the attic wasn't safe for drinking, and it fed into the bathrooms. The thought of going downstairs and bumping into my mother, though, made me choose to take my chances with the tap water.

I take one final glance at Wolf, who has his eyes closed again, before I slip out of the room. I don't have to walk far before a figure in a crisp, white uniform catches my eye—a maid, moving with purpose toward me. She glances at the empty pitcher in my hand, and without a word, she reaches out for it. I'm not used to people helping me, but it's something I could get used to. So when she takes the empty pitcher from my hands with a nod, I release it. She disappears out of sight. I'm not sure if I should wait or return to the room, but the chirp of my phone from the pocket of my dress distracts me. I fish it out of the small pocket along the thigh of my dress. The one thing I always ask for is for my garments to have pockets. The screen lights up with a message that instantly sends a shiver down my spine. It's from my mother.

"Where are you?" The text is brief, but I can hear her voice in it. Her voice is edged with that familiar blend of worry and disapproval. My fingers hover over the keyboard, my mind racing. How do I explain, yet again, that I am attending the most important yearly social event in our city? An event that, for better or worse, could shape my future and that of our family? She knows this, but with all the alcohol fueling her body, she's very forgetful.

I type out a response, reminding her of where I am.

No sooner have I sent the message than a reply comes through, and with it, a knot forms in my stomach.

"Whoring again." Her words lash through the phone. She's always been angry at me, but even more so since the loss of my brothers—a void that nothing can fill—has left her grappling with a depression so deep it colors every word she says to me. The absence of my youngest brother, Michael, who we only hear from through sporadic letters, adds to the constant fear that one day, those letters will stop coming.

But I shouldn't have to be her punching bag. That's all I am to her.

"No. Securing our family's future, Tess." I use her name for extra emphasis.

"Your water." I glance up at the maid, who has returned with the water, and I take it from her before making my way back to Wolf.

I slip the phone back into my pocket, a sense of resolve hardening within me. Today, proving myself to Diarmuid is more important than fighting with my mother.

With a deep breath, I lift my chin and step forward, ready to face whatever is behind this door. But my ringing phone has me pausing.

"Can I hold that for you?" The maid is still standing in the hallway. I want to tell her to leave, but instead, I hand her the pitcher and answer my mother's persistent rings.

"I'm busy, Mother," I say.

"Have you so easily forgotten about your brothers?" Her words are slurred and filled with pain. This week marks a painful anniversary—the death of Dominic, my older brother. The memory is a sharp, constant ache, a reminder of the price paid by those forced to serve the Hand of Kings. Dominic and Kevin, both lost to a cause they had no choice in, their futures snuffed out prematurely. Dominic's death, in particular—gunned down during a police raid—haunts our family, a wound that never truly heals. But I feel that pain, too.

The timing of the anniversary only serves to heighten my mother's volatility, a fact I'm painfully reminded of as she continues to spew her poison down the phone.

"Of course, you have forgotten. All Amira cares about is Amira."

I turn away from the maid and hiss into the phone. "I haven't forgotten. But you seem to forget you still have a daughter." I'm braver with the distance between us. If I were home, she would surely strike me. I don't want to go back to that house, to the suffocating atmosphere of sorrow and resentment.

"You're not much of a daughter." Her words lash out, and I end the call. The pain of her words is too much.

I turn to find the maid watching me. I slip the phone back into my pocket. I reach for the pitcher, but not before the maid's gaze meets mine, a flicker of concern in her eyes. It's a kindness, perhaps, but in that moment, it feels like pity, and something within me recoils.

"What are you looking at?" The words snap from my lips, sharper than I intended. It's a defense mechanism, an instinctual cover for the pain that's threatening to spill over. The maid, taken aback, merely hands me the pitcher and moves past me, her momentary concern replaced by a professional detachment.

I retreat to the guest room, only to find Wolf sitting up in bed, looking woozy but alert. He finishes a glass of water as I enter. When Wolf's gaze meets mine, I recognize something in his deep gray eyes. Like me, he carries his own pain. A shadow seems to cling to him, visible in the weariness of his eyes and the careful way he holds himself.

"Where is Diarmuid?" are his first words.

I place the pitcher on his bedside table. "I'm not sure," I answer honestly. "I think he's with Lorcan and Ronan."

He huffs at that. "I'm sure they are discussing what to do with me."

I hesitate, not sure how much to pry, but any opportunity to get to know Diarmuid better is one I will grab with both hands.

"They seemed very concerned when you fell." I lie remembering how Diarmuid had released Wolf in anger, allowing his cousin to fall and bang his head.

"They don't care about me." His words are bitter, and he takes another drink. "They would be glad if I were buried alongside my father."

"I doubt that is true," I respond.

He snorts. "You don't know my cousins." He waves his hand in the air. "You will soon enough, and then you will be running."

"He's been very kind to me," I say and think of how we shared a moment out in the garden. How he took my virginity from me and only me. He never touched Niamh or Selene, and why would he? They don't compare to me.

"Kind until he gets what he wants," Wolf says, watching me closely now.

He already got what he wanted, my mind sings. I shake the thought away.

A silence slips over the room for a moment.

"Who were you talking to on the phone? It seemed heated." Wolf sits up even further in the bed. He grows more alert by the minute.

I'm wondering how much I should share with him. "My mother," I answer.

Wolf doesn't pry, but I need to talk; I never talk about her. "It's our brother's anniversary—well, two of my brothers'—death. Michael…well… we aren't sure about him, to be honest." I find myself drifting to the end of the bed.

"I understand loss like that. I buried my father," Wolf says, with an almost vulnerable look in his gaze, but he doesn't have pity in his eyes, and that is what keeps me talking. I can't stand pity.

"I'm sorry about your father. It's a burden."

He nods in response.

"My brothers served the Hand of the Kings, also," I say and fold my hands onto my lap.

"Oh, I may have known them. What is your second name, Amira?"

The fact he knows my first, surprises me. My last name isn't a secret. "Reardon."

Wolf's eyes light up as if he recognizes the name, but he shakes his head. "I can't say I worked with them, but then again, I've worked with a lot of people, being a Duke." He offers a lazy smile.

"You're a Duke yourself," I tease, a smile playing at my lips as I think to myself that if things don't work out with Diarmuid, maybe, just maybe, being close to Wolf might save me from being stuck at home with my mother. He didn't seem as bad as people made him out to be. In fact, I could see myself liking Wolf.

He returns the smile with a wry twist of his lips. Wolf suddenly pushes to his feet, a bit unsteady but determined. "I have to get to work," he announces.

"Your work can wait for another day," I protest half-heartedly, intrigued by what could possibly demand his attention so urgently. There's a part of me that knows all too well the nature of his duties, yet being in the room with him makes me wonder how much is really true.

He pauses, considering something. "Why don't you come see my office?" He suggests a challenge in his eyes. I hesitate, aware of the reasons why such an action would be frowned upon. "It probably isn't appropriate for a Bride to be alone with another man," I murmur.

Wolf's response is immediate, confident. "I have nothing to hide from Diarmuid," he states, his tone leaving no room for argument.

The invitation hangs between us. I stand and consider his offer, the knowledge of what he does, the intrigue of the unknown, and the sheer boldness of his invitation stirring a reckless desire inside me.

The transition from the luxurious, suffocating atmosphere of the event to the starkness of the old school building is jarring. We hadn't far to go, just across the courtyard, before we arrived at what Wolf says is his office.

I'm reconsidering my decision, glancing back at the mansion with all its glistening lights. But as Wolf steps into the foyer, I find myself following him. The chill of the stone walls contrasts sharply with the warmth we've left behind, making me very aware of how scantily I'm dressed. The building, despite its seemingly abandoned exterior, exudes an air of careful maintenance. The wooden floors gleam under the steady glow of well-maintained lighting, free of the cobwebs one might expect in such a place. A calendar on the wall, its pages fresh and current, seems oddly out of place in the otherwise timeless space.

I can't help but feel a mixture of confusion and curiosity as we walk through the entrance. "This is not what I expected," I admit, my voice echoing slightly in the open space.

Wolf glances at me, a hint of amusement in his eyes. "The O'Sullivans have always been good at hiding in plain sight," he explains, his tone casual but carrying an undercurrent of seriousness. "Ever since they joined forces with the Hand of Kings, secrecy has become a cornerstone of their operations. Most of my dealings are through contacts within the Hand. Diarmuid's side of the business, given his involvement in the illegal arms trade, tends to work more closely with the O'Sullivan network."

The revelation of Diarmuid's activities, while shocking, doesn't surprise me as much as it should. Yet, hearing it spoken aloud by Wolf brings new clarity. Maybe Wolf has more power than Diarmuid if he works so closely with the Hand of the Kings.

As we move beyond the foyer, the facade of the old school continues to unravel, revealing its true purpose. The presence of regular offices makes this place almost seem mundane.

That is, until we step into Wolf's office. It's such a large, yet inviting room. The warmth radiates from a fire that has been kept lit for a while now. Off to the left is paned glass, hiding another room, but I can't make it out. The chill from walking across the courtyard starts to ease.

"There are things I know that could upset the ruling governments of most of the world powers," he states, a grim seriousness etching his features as he sits behind an old and oversized desk. He points at the chair in front of his desk for me to take.

My curiosity piques. "What kind of things?" I ask, not sure I'm ready for the answer.

"Disgusting, sinful things, Amira," he replies, his gaze fixed on a point somewhere beyond my head.

The gravity of his words sends a shiver down my spine, a realization of the depth and darkness of the secrets Wolf harbors. It's a reminder of the world I'm stepping into and also a reminder that I shouldn't be here.

He rises, and I'm surprised when he holds a hand up for me to stay seated. "Wait here."

I sit in the warm room and wonder where he has gone. It's not long before I get up, unease rippling through my system.

After what feels like an eternity, Wolf re-enters his expression unreadable. "What's going on?" I ask.

"I'm going to allow you to see me work," he answers, a cryptic smile playing at the edges of his lips.

He guides me to another door, this one secure with both analog and digital locks. Once through, we enter a room that stands in stark contrast to everything I've seen thus far.

"The sex training room," he states calmly, like that statement alone shouldn't have me running back to the safety of the manor.

He directs me to a chair in the corner of the room and tells me to wait. "I have this feeling you would like to see my work."

I can't answer. I'm curious what a sex training room is. Maybe I could learn something to use on Diarmuid to gain the upper hand. I know Wolf won't touch me—it's forbidden—so I nod and wait to see what he wants to show me.

"Have you seen anyone else arriving here?" he asks all of a sudden.

I shake my head. "No."

"At least a dozen people have seen you. This place has lots of secrets and a lot of protection, too. It has to."

The far door opens before I can respond or decipher what his words could mean. A young woman enters.

Wolf smiles kindly at the woman and signals her to approach him with two fingers.

She does with a bowed head. The dressing gown she wears covers her body, but I don't think she wears anything underneath it.

"The Dukes and Kings of the Hand of the Kings prefer virgins. But I know a woman has greater value if she has some experience." I sit up straighter.

He leads the woman to a chair, but before she sits down, she strips off her gown. Beneath it, she is naked like I thought.

Wolf stands behind her, his gaze never leaving mine. He runs both his hands down across her breasts and squeezes her nipples lightly. The woman's face is covered with her long, loose hair, and I want to see her eyes. But I don't dare speak as Wolf continues to play with her breasts. His strokes aren't gentle, and redness starts to grow along the skin from his constant grabbing. He's watching me as he rolls her nipples between his fingers and pulls them outward. I lick my lips, and he grins before he moves around her and kneels at her feet.

"It is my job to teach women how to be the best lovers possible before I marry them off or sell them." He states and spreads the woman's legs, revealing her private area. I'm surprised to see she has no pubic hair. I'm wondering if it's something Wolf prefers, or if the woman did it herself.

I have so many questions, like why wasn't I trained? Or what does he mean to sell them off? But the words are cut off as he runs his large hands up her thighs and spreads her legs as far as the chair will allow. He's left enough room so I can see as he slips a finger inside the woman, and she groans in pleasure. My stomach dances with butterflies. I'm back to looking at the woman's face, but I can't see with all the hair hanging loose.

"I want to see her eyes." I find the words.

He smiles with delight and reaches up, grabbing a bunch of her hair to yank her head back. Her oval face has creamy, flawless skin, her lips are slightly parted, and her bottom lip is large. Her white teeth are stark against her pink lips. She's very pretty. Would Diarmuid prefer her more than me? An unyielding anger has me wanting to hurt her, but I stay in my seat. Wolf slips another finger inside the woman. This time, his movements are harsh, and the woman hisses in what sounds like pain, and that makes me smile. He doesn't think she is prettier than me. He wouldn't dare touch me like that; it reminds me of my worth. I'm so much more than these whores.

When I meet Wolf's gaze, he smiles back at me. "Does this turn you on?" he asks as he continues to plow his fingers into the woman. He keeps a tight grip on her hair, never allowing it to cover her face, keeping the curtain back so I can watch the show.

"Yes," I whisper.

He nods. "There is no shame in that. You can learn by watching, but you can touch yourself if you wish."

I want to touch myself, but I also know the complications of my actions.

Wolf, as if noticing my hesitation, rises to his feet; the woman instantly pulls her legs together, and her annoying hair falls down around her face. Wolf gathers her hair again, and I'm surprised at how thoughtful he's being for me. He scoops it back in a low ponytail and uses his fingers as a tie. While looking at me, he unzips his pants, and his large cock springs free. He's still looking at me when he directs the woman's head to his cock by pulling her hair. She looks up at him with large eyes, but he isn't paying her attention. No, he's paying me attention.

"Circle your mouth and suck." He instructs her she reaches up, and I notice the shake in her hand as she places the tip of his cock in her mouth.

"Open wider," he commands, and she does.

He groans. "Watch those teeth; no man wants to feel your teeth." His words are gritted, and as he teaches the woman how to give him a blowjob, I grow wetter. The sounds of the woman's saliva and the sucking sounds along his cock has me squirming in my seat. I've never watched porn, never mind watching someone perform a sexual act in front of me. Not to this degree, anyway. With Selene and Niamh on our first night at the Hands of Kings' mansion, that was brief. Not like this at all.

Wolf continues to watch me, and his features morph into an ecstasy that I want a part in. He pushes his cock further down the woman's throat, and she's gagging, but he doesn't stop. His hand loosens around her hand and spreads out on the back of her head, restricting her from pulling away from his cock. With each ragged breath from him and each choking noise from her, I become braver.

I let my hand fall between my legs and gain access easily to my core beneath my short dress. I'm swollen with need and touch myself.

Wolf smiles. "Good girl. You can be my student, one I will never touch, but you can watch and learn."

The idea makes me wetter. I could learn and enjoy myself. The woman's face is puce as Wolf's movements grow frantic while he fucks her mouth with no mercy. My own fingers move quicker over my swollen bud. I want to come, but some part of me doesn't want this to end. The woman's hand reaches up and touches Wolf's torso as if she's getting ready to push him away, but something makes her drop her hands.

Wolf's groans fill the room, and when he slams into the woman's mouth, spit and his cum pours out of the corners, but he doesn't remove his cock. It's too much for me, and I come, sitting in the chair as the woman slaps his stomach, finally losing control as she tries to break free. Tears pour down her face. But Wolf isn't letting her go. Not even close.

Chapter Sixteen

Niamh

As the Hand of Kings' car pulls up to my family's stately home, the silence of the night wraps around me like a cloak. I expect anger, worry, perhaps a lecture waiting at the doorstep. But there's none. Instead, when my father shuffles to the door, wrapped in his bathrobe, his face lights up with a smile so warm it feels out of place in the cool night air.

"Ah, Niamh, you're back," he says, his voice laced with a giddiness that makes my stomach churn. I know immediately what he's thinking—his assumptions about Diarmuid and me, about what my absence signifies. I bite my lip, wondering how his expression might change if he knew the truth. That my night had been spent in an entirely different company than what he'd approve of.

"Goodnight, Dad," I manage, stepping past him before the questions start.

"Oh, goodnight, love." His cheeriness makes my shoulders tip closer to my chest. No father should be happy when their daughter comes home so late, but the fact that he isn't asking questions makes me climb the stairs quickly.

As I make my way to my room, the sight of Ella's door catches my eye. My heart aches with the need to see her. My hand hovers over the wood, longing to feel the warmth of her presence, to hear her sleepy voice tell me everything is okay. But I stop. She's been run ragged by Mom's insistence on perfection between school and ballet, and she deserves her rest. With a heavy heart, I retreat.

Once inside my room, the mirror catches my reflection. Selene's choice in the dress I'm still wearing shines under the moonlight filtering through the windows. She has an eye for fashion that could make anyone feel beautiful, even when their world is quietly crumbling. I promise myself to thank her, to let her know her efforts didn't go unnoticed.

But as I peel off the layers of silk and lace, my thoughts drift back to Ella. Panic rises within me, a familiar, unwelcome guest. My father's assumptions about Diarmuid couldn't be further from the truth. Amira, with her perfect timing and sharper instincts, had swept in before I had the chance. Not that I was playing the same game. My stakes are different; they're personal. They're Ella. She needs me to be strong to succeed where it truly matters.

My mind races, and the sudden ring of my old phone slices through the silence of my room like a beacon in the dark. I race to the bedside table and glance at the screen. It's Selene. My heart skips a beat, part hope, part dread. What does she want? Could this be about Amira? Or something else entirely?

I brace myself and answer. Having a backup phone with my original number was my mother's doing. She insists we always have a backup. I keep it charged but barely use the older model.

"Ay, Niamh! I'm sorry to disturb you. I just want to know the name of that guy you met in the woods. Not just the name. The number. I need the number," she rushes out, her words tumbling over each other.

My brow furrows in confusion, the fatigue from the night's events making it hard to keep up. "Selene? I don't understand. Why—" I begin, but she cuts me off, her urgency palpable even through the phone.

"—we agreed to help this woman and we are. We need to. Someone is looking for her," she explains, her voice a mix of determination and worry.

"Selene, it's getting late," I protest weakly, hoping to push this conversation to morning so I don't wake up Ella; I walk to my bedroom door and make sure it's closed tight.

But Selene is relentless. "Text him, then. Tell him we will be there tomorrow morning," she insists, leaving no room for argument.

I sigh, running a hand through my hair, the events of the night catching up to me all at once. With a nod to myself, even though she can't see it, I agree. "Okay, Selene. I'll do it now. We'll sort this out."

I end the call, the room falls silent once more, and I scoop the card out of my dress pocket. I still need to replace my new phone, another thing I'll add to my list of things to do. I quickly type out a message to Rian. Despite the exhaustion tugging at my limbs, a sense of purpose steadies my heart. We had made a promise to help and help we would.

The morning light creeps through my curtains, painting my room with the soft hues of dawn. I wake with a flutter of excitement in my chest, a rare feeling these days, spurred by the thought of spending a few precious moments with Ella before the day fully begins. But as I pass by her room, my heart sinks. Her bed is neatly made, empty, the lingering scent of her perfume the only sign she was ever there. She must have left early for class, another reminder of the space growing between us.

I return to my room and get dressed quickly. Rian had agreed to meet me and Selene this morning at his apartment. After slipping on a pair of jeans and a cream-colored sweater, I tie my sandy hair up with a hair tie and wash up in the bathroom before I enter the kitchen. Breakfast is a quiet affair, my thoughts still lingering on Ella and the day ahead. I break the silence. "I have to go off this morning," I say, breaking a croissant in half.

My mother gives my breakfast a disapproving glare. She normally only allows me to have fruit in the mornings, but since I'm not under her strict eating rules, I enjoy the pastry in front of me. I have no idea why we have so much if we can't eat it.

I'm expecting a load of questions. Instead, my announcement is met with an outpouring of pride and excitement. Their eyes shine, not with the joy of my accomplishments or happiness, but with the reflection of their own desires. They see me not as their daughter but as a key to unlocking the life of luxury and ease they've always craved, a life they believe marrying into royalty can provide. The weight of their expectations sits heavily on my shoulders, a crown of thorns disguised as gold. My appetite dwindles as my father reaches across and takes my mother's hand, a silent message that things are going their way.

"We have a guest at the door," The maid informs us all. I rise quickly, gather my old phone, and stuff it into my pocket before anyone notices and wonders what happened to my new slick phone.

My father rises, too. "Best meet the man in question." My father is dressed in a suit and proudly pushes back his shoulders.

I can't help but stifle a laugh at the sheer disappointment etched across my father's face. His dreams of Kings and grandeur were momentarily shattered by the arrival of a friend, not a suitor.

"Father, this is Selene McNamara," I say.

He covers his disappointment quickly and takes Selene's hand, giving it a firm shake. Before he asks any questions, I grab a coat off the hook and link my arm with Selene's. "I'll be back later." We race from the house and walk down the driveway out onto the road.

"Your father seems nice," Selene says, glancing back over her shoulder.

"He's still watching," I reply without looking back.

"Yes." Selene frowns, and I tug her to the left, out of sight.

"He thought Diarmuid was coming to get me this morning." I offer up the explanation to her that she hadn't asked for.

At the mention of Diarmuid's name, Selene tenses.

We walk the rest of the way to the bus stop in silence. Only a few people are waiting, and we arrive just in time as the bus pulls up. Selene gets two tickets for Sandyford, and we find a seat.

The bus ride to Sandyford is filled with an uneasy silence, broken only by my inquiry into Selene's unusual determination.

"Did something else happen?" I whisper, not wanting anyone else to hear our conversation.

Selene's features tighten. "No. I just want to help."

She isn't telling me everything and seems unwilling to talk this morning. So, I leave her alone and glance out the window. As the cityscape blurs past the window, I realize that perhaps, for Selene, this is more than just solving a crime; maybe it's a way to take control in a world where we truly have none.

When we finally arrive at Rian's place, I'm not sure what I was expecting, but it certainly isn't this. The building itself is one of those new, nondescript blocks that seem to have sprung up overnight to cater to the city's ever-desperate demand for living space. It's clear from the get-go that Rian's apartment, like many others here, was designed with functionality in mind over comfort, intended for those willing to compromise space for a place to call home.

Stepping inside, the contrast is startling. Every inch of Rian's studio apartment is consumed by his work. The walls are plastered with photographs, notes, and maps, all connected by a spiderweb of strings that trace patterns only he could decipher. Timelines stretch across the walls, and stacks of books and papers clutter every available surface, creating a chaos that's both bewildering and strangely ordered. A single corner stands out in stark contrast—clean and carefully arranged, the dedicated space for his video podcasts, a slice of normalcy in a room swallowed by obsession.

Selene's voice cuts through my initial shock, her words tinged with dark humor. "Feels like we've stepped into the den of a serial killer, doesn't it?" she comments, and despite the gravity of our visit, I can't help but let out a laugh. The tension in the room lightens, just a fraction, as Rian turns to greet us with an energy and warmth that's immediately disarming. He pushes his glasses up on his nose as he smiles warmly at us.

I can't help but smile back; his open and friendly approach makes me trust him. I glance at Selene. She's more guarded.

"We wanted to talk about Andrew O'Sullivan," Selene starts. Rian isn't put off by the instant jump to why we are here.

The moment the name is mentioned, Rian springs into action, adding another string to his complex web of information—the physical connection of string to pin, linking Andrew O'Sullivan to the woman.

"Do we know who the woman is?" Selene's question weighs heavier than anything else in the room; that's why we are here, after all.

Rian speaks with a confidence that's both reassuring and concerning. "No, not yet. But the best lead we have is through the medical examiner's office," he asserts, his eyes scanning his network of clues as if they might reveal a new path at any moment.

Selene's interest piques at this, her mind already racing ahead to the logistics. "Do you have any fake IDs or something that could get us in?" she asks, her voice a blend of hope and practicality.

Rian shakes his head, a rueful smile playing on his lips. "No, nothing like that. But, if the body is being claimed by a possible family member, there might be a way to gather enough information to aid our investigation without needing to sneak in." He moves to a small fridge and extracts three frubes, offering one to me and the other to Selene. I decline again, just like I did the day I met him, and he doesn't seem put off as Selene declines, too, with the curl of her nose. I'm not sure how he can eat when we are talking about a dead body.

"Why does milk turn into yogurt when you take it to a museum?" Rian reads the joke before he rips off the top of the plastic.

"I don't know," Selene says.

"I'm intrigued," I say.

Rian smiles. "Because it turns into cultured milk."

As he drinks his yogurt, I try to get us back on track.

"You do realize that getting involved with this could be dangerous for you, right?" I warn him, hoping he understands the gravity of our situation. I'm saying it for me and Selene also.

"I don't care about the danger," he says, his focus unwavering. It's clear that the pursuit of truth, the unraveling of this mystery, outweighs any personal risk in his mind.

"Okay, so you can go in then?" I ask.

"Oh no, they know who I am; I could never get in. You two will be going in by yourselves," Rian states matter-of-factly.

His words settle over us. I want to protest that this is getting out of hand.

I look over at Selene, ready to protest, ready to turn and leave. We can forget we ever started down this path. We can remain ignorant.

We can remain safe.

But something gleams in Selene's eyes. Determination. A grim kind of resolution. Her gaze flickers to mine, and when she speaks, I find myself nodding despite my fears.

We're in."

CHAPTER SEVENTEEN

DIARMUID

A S I WALK THROUGH the hallowed halls of St. Gertrude's Church, the air vibrates with the harmonious singing of the choir. Their voices lift and soar, reverberating against the ancient stone walls. I tread lightly between the altars, my steps measured, my heart attuned to the sanctity of this place. Pausing at the transept, where the architecture of the church forms the solemn shape of the cross, I feel a moment of reverence, and my mind sings that we should all burst into flames for our sins. I turn away, hating how much control the church—or, more precisely, Victor—has over us all.

Beyond the reach of the choir's celestial sounds lie the hidden chancel, shrouded in thick, velvet curtains. Behind the far right curtain, shielded from view, I can hear whispers that get swallowed up amidst the choir's song. In this moment, I'm reminded of tales of secret societies, of hidden truths and ancient mysteries—a feeling akin to stepping into a scene from *Angels & Demons* or

The Da Vinci Code. The intrigue that surrounds these hidden chapels stirs a sense of anticipation within me, hinting at the depths of the organization's reach, perhaps as far-reaching as the tunnels beneath Newgrange.

I'm not alone in the church; the choir members' voices are not the only presence here. Floor sweepers, altar polishers, and light duster all move through the space with a purpose. Their tasks are seemingly mundane yet vital to the preservation of this sacred environment. Victor, ever the strategist, leaves nothing to chance.

Slipping through the heavy velvet curtain, I enter the concealed chancel. The space closes behind me with a hush, the fabric falling into place. My eyes adjust to the dim light, and the figures before me come into sharp focus. Lorcan, Ronan, Wolf, Victor, and there, like a shadow from my past, Oisin Cormick. Oisin, the killer who guided my hands to become what they are today. The sight of him, especially next to Victor, sends a shiver through me, unearthing memories long buried.

A memory flashes before my eyes, unbidden yet vivid. I'm eleven, witnessing the execution of a woman for the first time. Until then, death had been a distant concept, one I executed without personal connection, and always men. But her scream—it pierced the air. She was a prisoner; her crimes justified her fate in the eyes of our laws, but the reality of her death shook me to my core. She had killed her husband and brother all in the name of money. As she screamed for death, I had turned away, unable to watch, a moment of weakness that didn't go unnoticed. Cormick had seen, and he had reported it.

The aftermath of that day is a blur of pain and reprimand. Two figures loomed large in my punishment: Victor, with his cold disappointment, and Uncle Andrew, a man whose anger was both swift and brutal: punches, kicks, the unforgiving hardness of walls against my back. The air was filled with shouts, the sound of objects breaking, thrown in a rage meant to discipline, to harden. Those moments shaped me, molded me into the weapon I am, yet left scars no one can see, scars that ache when the past surfaces.

As I stand among them now, the weight of those long-ago punishments heavy in the air around me, I remember the lessons disguised as torture. Victor's method was always precise and calculated to teach endurance and control. The memory of the candle's flame flickers in my mind, its heat a ghost on my skin. I was made to hold my hand just above it, the fire close enough to singe, to warn of the pain that comes with failure. Each instinctive recoil, each flinch away from the heat, was met with the sharp lash of Victor's whip across my back. The scars that web my skin are hidden relics of those lessons, marks of a past I carry with me. They are a part of me no one has seen, secrets kept even from my Brides.

Despite the turmoil within, I manage to compose myself, taking a seat calmly beside Lorcan. The contrast between the tranquility of my outward appearance and the storm of my memories is stark. Around us, the conversation shifts, a momentary distraction from the path of reflection.

"The choir sings ever so beautifully," Oisin remarks.

Victor, however, is quick to critique, his ear finding fault where others find beauty. "They are flat," he declares, his voice devoid of warmth.

Victor stands at the helm of our gathering, his authority unchallenged, his command absolute. Previous meetings with my brothers, filled with the casual back-and-forth of familial bonds and rivalry, now serve as stark contrasts to this moment. Here, in Victor's presence, no one dares interrupt. No one dares to contradict. The respect—or perhaps fear—he commands is palpable, suffocating. Despite the rage simmering within me, a desire to smash his head against the cold marble, I remain still.

Oisin's presence complicates matters further. The man molded me, but he's retired, so I have no idea what he's doing here.

Victor's voice cuts through the silence, drawing my focus.

"The investigation into Andrew O'Sullivan's murder has revealed no more leads. The Gardai have been ineffective in their search. Whether due to incompetence or corruption, they are no further on." He glances at each of us.

"We need answers, actions. This can't be ignored."

Victor places his hands behind his back, tilting his head up and looking at the ceiling before giving each of us a sharp look. "That is why I've pulled Oisin out of retirement."

Everything in me freezes. This is the last action I thought Victor would take, especially since he suspects me.

The very idea that the man from whom I learned everything is now an active player changes everything.

Victor glances at Oisin. "Failure is not an option."

I try to keep my features relaxed, but my heart races in my chest. I glance at Wolf, who is delighted with this news.

I can't afford even the tiniest slip up. Selene's earlier accusations about me being a hitman crash heavily against my skull. No matter if the information is something she pieced together or was told, I need to make sure my Brides are in line at all times. One tiny slip up from here on out could cost me my head.

"You will all work closely with Oisin. Whatever he needs from you, you will grant." We all nod, but Victor's gaze lingers on me.

I hate him with so much passion. I will have my moment to destroy him, but for right now, I need to think of a way that he doesn't destroy me first.

Chapter Eighteen
Selene

T HE RED BRICK BUILDING towers over us, its grandeur reminding me more of a castle than the coroner's office. Despite its apparent age, I know it's a fairly new construction. The sweeping driveway leading up to it is deserted except for us.

I adjust my stride to match Niamh's erratic pacing. She bumps into me yet again, a little too hard this time, causing me to stumble slightly. I glance at her, puzzled by her inability to walk in a straight line despite being perfectly sober. This may be all too much for her, especially since Rian shared more information with us that he was holding onto.

The girl who was found on top of Andrew's grave has brown curly hair. It's such a small detail, but for both of us, it's starting to paint a picture, especially since we have a photo of a missing girl who doesn't appear to even be eighteen.

"Niamh, are you okay?" I ask, keeping my voice low despite the emptiness around us. It feels like the walls have ears, and the last thing we need is unwanted attention.

She gives me a tight-lipped smile, her eyes darting around nervously. "Just, I want this done and over with."

I can't help but agree. It was the mushroom pickers who had found the body. They told Rian the details of what they found, and we have one more final detail. She was wearing a tweed jacket on the twenty-second day of September.

As we reach the grand front door, Niamh straightens up. She rings the bell, and the sound echoes, seemingly swallowed by the building's vast interior. Moments later, the door swings open to reveal a stern-faced woman in a coroner's uniform.

"Can I help you?" she asks, her tone as cold as the air that flows out from the building. All the dead people are in there. I swallow, ready to speak, but Niamh seems to have found her nerve.

Niamh steps forward, and I admire her courage as she speaks. "Yes, we believe we may be related to a woman who was found on September 22nd. We were hoping to... to claim her, if possible."

The woman's expression softens slightly, but she maintains her professional demeanor. "I see. Do you have any proof of your relationship? Anything at all that can help us verify your claim?"

Niamh and I exchange a glance. This is the part we hadn't fully prepared for.

"We... we have this," I say, pulling out a photograph from my jacket pocket. My fingers are sweaty around the image. I find it hard to look at the young, smiling girl that Rian had somehow dug up from the internet. He must have spent hours comparing the small details he had gathered to find a girl who matched this description and who had been declared missing in this area on September 22nd.

The coroner studies the photograph, then us, her gaze lingering a little too long on our faces. "Do you have any ID?" She finally says.

Shit. Of course, she would ask for ID. I curse Rian for not thinking of this; I curse myself, too.

"We got here as quick as we could; I'm sorry, I don't." I hang my head and take a large lungful of air.

"She always wore her tweed jacket around this time of year. It was her favorite." I hope sharing this knowledge will prove that we know her.

The assistant still watches me. I don't know what she sees on our faces, but all of a sudden, she's hesitant.

No.

Niamh chimes in, her voice stronger than I've heard it today. "We got a letter from her two years ago, but nothing since. We've been so worried. Please, we just need to know if that's her."

The assistant nods, seemingly swayed by Niamh. "Let me check the records for the clothing description." She steps away, leaving us to wait at the reception desk.

The wait stretches out like a long, dark alleyway in front of us. Niamh doesn't speak, and I don't try to engage in conversation. If I do, I might end up convincing us to leave.

The assistant returns.

"Normally I need ID, but there's something about your request... Follow me."

As we step into the building, I can't help but feel like we've just crossed an invisible threshold. The interior is just as imposing as the exterior, with high ceilings and long, echoing corridors. My heart races with a mixture of fear and anticipation. What are we about to discover? And more importantly, are we ready for the truth that awaits us?

The coroner's assistant leads us down a long, sterile hallway, her steps echoing off the walls, adding a somber rhythm to our procession. The air is thick with a blend of disinfectant and something else, something I can't pinpoint. Niamh's hand brushes against mine. Her features are strained, and she does appear to be a grieving sister. I think she is imagining her own sister on a slab. I know they are close.

My heart pounds in my chest, a frantic drumbeat as we draw closer to the room, and the reality that I'm going to see a dead body that isn't painted for the Gods or clothed for the living sets in. It will be raw, white, and appear very much dead.

We're shown into a small, stark room. The assistant pauses at the door, her face unreadable. "I'll need a moment to prepare," she says before leaving us alone with our thoughts and our fears.

Niamh turns to me, her face pale under the harsh fluorescent lights. "Do you think we're doing the right thing?" She whispers, her voice barely carrying across the room.

I clutch the photograph tighter, the edges wrinkling under the pressure. I glance down at the picture. The girl has the kind of ordinary face that blends into the crowd.

"We're too far in to doubt ourselves now," I reply, my voice steadier than I feel. "Remember, Megan ran away because of that boyfriend right before graduation. That's our story."

Niamh nods, biting her lip, the anxiety clear in her eyes. But there's also resolve there, a determination that mirrors my own.

When the assistant returns, she doesn't waste time on pleasantries. "Follow me," is all she says, leading us to another room, this one with a somber purpose. The air is colder here, the kind of cold that seeps into your bones.

She stops by a table that's covered with a sheet, her expression softening just a tad. "We're not allowed to do this usually, but something about your story..." She trails off, leaving the sentence hanging in the cold air.

Niamh squeezes my hand, her presence a comforting anchor in the storm of my thoughts. I'm thinking we could just peek under the sheet and leave. I glance at Niamh, who's watching the door.

I want to know what lies under that sheet, but it also terrifies me.

"The body... she was found wearing a tweed jacket," she starts, and for a moment, the world seems to stop spinning.

The revelation hits us like a physical blow. As the assistant prepares to reveal the body, I brace myself, not just for the possibility of recognizing the girl from the photo but for the consequences of today.

The assistant, with a solemn nod, carefully pulls back the sheet. My heart races, but I force myself to look. Niamh, on the other hand, can't bear it. She turns away instantly, burying her head in my shoulder. Her reaction, while genuine in its horror, fits perfectly with what the assistant would expect.

The girl on the table is indeed young, her features peaceful yet hauntingly still, marred only by the stark, unnatural bruising around her neck. The discoloration stands out, a silent testament to the struggle that marked her final moments. It's jarring, and my calm façade begins to crack under the weight of this visible violence.

"The coroner is ruling it as suicide," the assistant says, her voice steady but lacking conviction.

I can't help myself; my gaze flicks to the assistant, searching her face for any sign of doubt, and I find it. There's a hesitation in her eyes, a flicker of uncertainty.

I need her to talk. We have come this far. "She would never have taken her life," I say. My gaze wavers with guilt at seeing this girl's body. A part of me knows we have no right to see her in such a state.

She hesitates, glancing at the door. "It's just that... the bruising, the positioning. It doesn't sit right with me," she confesses in a hushed tone. "But I'm not the coroner. I just assist."

"But you've seen things that don't add up," I press, my resolve hardening. "Things that might suggest... something else?"

She looks torn, caught between her professional duty and the truth she must suspect. "I can't say for sure. There are just... doubts. The angle of the bruising, the lack of other injuries... It's as if she was...," she trails off, unable to finish the thought.

I nod, but Niamh squeezes my shoulder as if to tell me we have to go. The bruising around her neck speaks of a struggle.

The sheet is placed back over the girl, and the assistant steps away.

Niamh lifts her head from my shoulder, her eyes red but determined. "What do we do now?" She whispers, her voice barely audible.

"We find the truth," I reply, my voice laced with a newfound determination. "For her and for all the Megans out there whose stories don't end as neatly as they're told."

The assistant returns to us, chewing her lip. Lowering her voice to a whisper. "There was skin found beneath her fingernails," she divulges, glancing nervously around as if the walls themselves might be listening. "The coroner tested it and claimed it matched her own DNA. Said it wasn't from an assailant."

I process her words, the implication sending a cold shiver down my spine. The absence of scratch marks on her body—it doesn't add up. She hadn't been clawing at herself in a frenzied attempt to escape some inner torment. No, she had been fighting for her life, grappling with a very real and external threat.

"She didn't scratch herself," I mutter, more to myself than to Niamh or the assistant. "She scratched the person who killed her." The words taste bitter in my mouth, a vile truth hidden beneath layers of convenient lies.

Niamh's grip on my arm tightens. A wave of nausea washes over me, the room spinning as the reality of what we're suggesting settles in. I clamp a hand over my mouth, fighting back the urge to vomit right there on the coroner's pristine floor.

The assistant mistakes my physical reaction for emotional turmoil, which, in a way, isn't entirely wrong. She quickly offers me a tissue, her eyes filled with a mix of sympathy and concern. "I'm sorry; this must be incredibly hard for you," she says, her voice gentle.

Gathering my composure, I take the tissue, using it more as a prop to cover my moment of weakness. "I... I can't be sure this is my sister," I stammer, playing back into our narrative with a thread of truth.

The assistant nods, understanding—or believing she understands—our plight. "We have a composite sketch," she offers. "An investigator tried to piece together what she might have looked like before... before she ended up here."

She retrieves the sketch from a folder and hands it over. The drawing depicts a young woman, vibrant and full of life, a stark contrast to the cold, silent form on the table. It's a glimpse into what could have been, a life cut tragically short.

Niamh and I lean in, studying the sketch. It's generic enough to be anyone, and yet, in the lines and shadows, I see the faces of every missing person, every unsolved case.

"Thank you," I say softly, handing back the sketch. "This... This helps, but I don't think it's our sister."

As we put distance between ourselves and the building that now seems more like a facade for darker truths, the reality of our situation settles in. The coroner's too-quick judgment and the ignored evidence, it all points to something sinister—a network of power and silence, possibly the mafia, a cult, or a terrifying mix of both.

"Are you okay?" I ask Niamh beside me.

"I can't stop thinking…what if that was Ella." Her lip wobbles.

I link my arm with hers. "It's not." I remind her.

She nods, but the heaviness in her gaze doesn't lift.

I take out my cell and call Rian. I relay everything we have learned.

"What's next is the most tedious job you'll ever do: figuring out who that is in the sketch," he says, a heavy sigh punctuating his words.

After ending the call, I turn to Niamh, who looks as if she's carrying the weight of the world on her shoulders. "All we have to do," I begin, my voice steady despite the turmoil within, "is to steadily chip away at this case. We give Diarmuid no reason to suspect what we've been up to."

Niamh nods, her eyes meeting mine with a renewed spark of determination. "One step at a time," she agrees, a semblance of a plan forming between us. "We stay under the radar, gather what we can, and build our case. For her," she adds, a vow to the girl in the sketch and all those like her who have been silenced too soon.

CHAPTER NINETEEN
DIARMUID

Tonight, I want to get to know my Brides on a more personal basis. I've ordered them to be waiting for me in the main bedroom. I shake off all the earlier tension, all the secrets I carry, and shed it all like a second skin at the door. Tonight will just be about fun.

As I enter the room, Selene and Niamh are already there. Both are wearing their gowns over the lingerie I selected for tonight, their gazes shielded, and I know they have bonded. I wonder if Selene shared what happened between us the last time, along with the knowledge she had acquired about me being a hitman. I remember her talking to the priest, Isaac, and he may have planted seeds in her head.

I offer a polite smile to try and break some of the tension. Niamh offers one back; Selene doesn't. She's still mad. I internally smile. I'd pegged her as a troublemaker from the second I laid eyes on her, and I'm correct. But by taking what I wanted from her the other night, I hoped it showed her she cannot fight this.

Amira walks in, her gaze flitting around the room. It skims past Selene and Niamh in disgust before landing on the table that I had brought in here by the staff. Light refreshments line the table.

"It's wonderful to see you all here," I say, my voice steady. "Please take a seat." I pull out each chair for them. Selene and Niamh sit together, and Amira sits beside me. She raises her chin high like she's seated where she should be.

I've spent time with each of them, and yet tonight, I have the urge for more. "Let's make this evening count," I propose, raising my glass in a toast.

Each of them picks up their glasses and takes a drink. Amira's dressing gown is slightly open, showing me a tantalizing flash of her flesh. She places her hand on my thigh with a coy smile on her painted-red lips.

My cock grows instantly, but I don't just want one tonight. I want to explore all three.

No one has touched the soft pastries, but I'm not interested in them either. They are just a way to relax my Brides.

Amira's hand trails up my chest until she touches my cheek very boldly. I don't stop her as she turns my face to hers and presses a kiss to my lips. Her tongue flicks into my mouth, and I suck it, causing a groan to slip from between her lips.

I turn my face away to find Niamh watching me with curiosity. That's all I need. I rise, not trying to adjust the erection prodding through my navy trousers. I walk to Niamh and hold out a hand. She glances at Selene as if for permission, and that annoys me, but she places her small hand into mine, and I pull her from her seat.

"You're very beautiful," I say.

Her brown eyes widen with surprise, and I reach back, unclipping her long sandy hair, letting it fall down her back. As I take off her dressing gown, I address Selene and Amira. "You are all beautiful." And so they are. Each one is as stunning as the other.

Niamh's dressing gown pools at her feet, and she steps away, showing me the sexy black lingerie that's sculpted to her body.

Her breasts are perfect, and the flimsy see-through fabric doesn't hide her hardened nipples. I reach up and brush my hand across the hard tips. Her tongue flicks out, and she wets her lips. I smile and lead her to the large bed.

"You can join us," I say to Amira and Selene.

Amira doesn't need me to say it twice; she's already peeled off her dressing gown and disposed of her underpants before she kneels in the center of the bed. Her boldness makes me reach out to her, and I press a kiss to her lips that she sinks into. I turn my head to Niamh and kiss her soft lips. Her kisses are more reserved than Amira's, but I sense a curiosity in how she moves her lips across mine.

Selene finally stands at the foot of the bed. "Remove your gown," I order.

Fire sparks in her eyes, but she does as I say. Her breasts are the largest, and her wide blue eyes reveal so much her mouth doesn't say. She doesn't trust me. It's clear. I hold out my hand to her, and she takes it as I lead her up onto the bed. With my three Brides surrounding me, I take my time and run my hands along their perfectly sculpted bodies.

Amira runs her hands along my back and grips my suit jacket, pulling it off. I allow her as I kiss Selene. I brush my tongue along her lips, demanding they part. When they don't, I run my fingers between her thighs, and she groans, giving me access to her mouth. Does she remember I finger fucked her and licked my fingers after? She tastes sweet, just like the wine she sipped on at the table. I turn my head and find Niamh with wide brown eyes watching me. Gripping the back of her neck, I drag her face to mine and kiss her gently on the lips.

Amira is still demanding my attention, her arms circling my waist. I've already had her, but I turn, and she immediately plows her tongue into my mouth, her movements daring and sending my temperature sky-rocketing. When her fingers start to work on the buttons of my shirt, I grip both her hands and stop her. That's one thing I won't allow. I won't remove my shirt.

She frowns, but I push her back until she's lying on the bed.

"Join her." I command Selene and Niamh. Once again, Selene is the last to follow my command. I will definitely have to revisit her home and teach her some manners. But for now, I'll enjoy them. As they lie on their backs, I get off the bed and remove my trousers and boxers. My cock is rock hard, and the thought of fucking the three of them has me climbing back up on the bed.

"Spread your legs," I say to all of them.

I taste Amira first while running my hands along Niamh's thighs. I work my way up until I push past her panties and find her folds pushing them apart. My tongue sinks into Amira's pussy, and her hands find my hair and push my head down greedily.

I work a finger inside Niamh, and she arches higher as if her body demands more. I push a second finger in as Amira grinds her pussy into my face. When I rise, my face is wet. I shift on the bed, swapping my hand over so I can still finger Niamh and taste Selene. Selene watches me, and I grin as I push her panties aside and lick along the outside of her folds. She doesn't groan until my tongue flicks across her clit. Only then does she give in.

Movement at my side has me licking Selene heavier as Amira's sweet mouth captures my cock. She spits on it before she starts to suck. I push my fingers deeper inside Niamh and consider placing a third in her, but Selene's sweet pussy demands my attention. Amira's lips touch the base of my cock, and then she's taking all of me in her mouth. Her suction is perfect, and if she keeps going, I'll end up coming.

Niamh arches again, her core tightening around my fingers, and I remove them and rise from in between Selene's legs. Amira releases my cock and quickly moves behind me as I rise to my knees. Her tongue laps my balls, and I close my eyes for a moment at the glorious sensation.

Niamh's gaze is bewildered, and when I reach down and yank her body to mine, she gives a little startled cry. Pushing her legs as far as they will go, I place the head of my cock at her opening. She tenses almost immediately. Leaning over her, I don't enter her body but press a wet kiss to her mouth, my hands moving along her swan-like neck. She rolls her head in pleasure, her hips rising as she seeks my cock. Amira continues to suck my balls, and I glance at Selene, who watches it all, her guard slowly coming down, lust shining heavily in her eyes.

I push the tip of my cock into Niamh and tighten my hold on her neck. Pain mixed with pleasure is an experience everyone should have. Niamh reaches up and covers her hands with mine, but I don't release as I push fully inside her. I start to tighten my grip, not hard enough to cut off her air supply, but a threat hangs there that I suspect will heighten her orgasm when she comes.

The moment my cock is fully inside Niamh with my hands gently encircling her neck, something shifts in her gaze. Her reaction is immediate; she's clawing at me in a searing panic, her eyes wild. Her legs kick under me. It takes me a moment to retract my hands, and from her neck, but she doesn't calm down.

She's scurrying away from me; her legs slam together as she fights for air. Amira continues to lick my balls as if not noticing Niamh's distress.

"Stop," I order.

Selene has reached Niamh and grabs her arm. "Take a breath." Tears pour down Niamh's face. I have no fucking idea what is happening, but a wave of protectiveness washes over me, mingling with guilt. This was not what I intended.

I slowly reach for Niamh, but she recoils from my touch, and I won't have that. I grip her face, making her look at me. "You're okay," I say.

"Take a deep breath, in through your nose, out through your mouth," Selene instructs.

Niamh starts to calm down, but fear is still etched into her features.

As I watch Selene soothe Niamh, I'm struck by the depth of my own feelings for these women, particularly for Niamh. It's a realization that comes with a weight of responsibility I hadn't fully acknowledged until now. I had sought to create an environment where barriers could be lowered, not realizing that in doing so, I might inadvertently expose wounds I knew nothing about.

What has frightened Niamh so much? "I would never hurt you," I reassure her.

It's then I notice Amira standing at the side of the bed, her dressing gown back on her body and a look of pure displeasure on her face.

Niamh continues to huddle in a corner of the bed. She looks more like a scared animal than the vibrant person I know her to be. Selene holds her and rubs her hair; it calms Niamh down. I scoot off the bed and get dressed.

"Let's get dressed," I suggest gently, my voice aiming to bridge the gap between us. "It'll make everything feel a bit more normal, right?"

Selene rolls her eyes, but there's a glimmer of understanding there. "Because clothes make everything better," she says, sarcasm lacing her tone, yet she moves to do as I suggest.

I kneel beside Niamh, offering a smile that I hope conveys sincerity. "You're safe here," I tell her, my voice soft but firm. "Nothing is going to happen to you." It's a promise, an oath I intend to keep.

Selene, pulling on her dressing gown, snorts. "Well, at least until Diarmuid picks his Consort. Then all bets are off."

I shake my head, meeting Niamh's gaze. "That's not true. My priority is to keep you all safe, always." It's a declaration made not just to Niamh, but to Selene as well, a vow against the fears that haunt their thoughts.

Amira enters the line of my sight. Her expression has hardened. "Safe? How can anyone be safe here?" Her voice is laced with skepticism, her eyes scanning the room and landing on Niamh with a disquieting intensity.

"Amira," I warn, not wanting to see Niamh worked up again.

My tone is sharp, sharp enough to cut through Amira's pouting.

A smile grows on her face. "Maybe Niamh can go home so Selene and I can pleasure you."

I stand, my decision clear. "Amira, you need to leave," I command.

She laughs, a sound devoid of any humor. "Make me."

She pushes too hard. Selene has returned to Niamh and helps her cover herself with her dressing gown. I reach across and grip Amira's arm, removing her from the room.

Once in the corridor, her actions caught me off guard. Her lips are on mine, her tears mingling with a kiss that's more desperation than desire. "I'm not afraid," she whispers between sobs, her words punctuated by the press of her body against mine. "Do whatever you want to me. Nothing can make me afraid."

"Amira," I start, my voice barely a whisper. "It's not about fear. It's about respect, about choices. I want you to feel safe, not because you think there's nothing left to lose, but because you truly are safe."

The air between us crackles with an intensity that's hard to breathe around. Amira's eyes are wild, her emotions refusing to be calmed. "I am not doing anything until Niamh is okay," I state firmly, my decision unyielding. It's a line drawn in the sand, a declaration of where my priorities lie.

Amira's reaction is instantaneous, a fury unleashed. She screams, a sound that echoes off the walls, filled with pain and anger and something else—desperation. Her nails find my cheek, a sharp, stinging sensation that's quickly followed by the warm trickle of blood.

The commotion draws the manse's workers, curious and concerned, to our floor. Their presence only adds to the chaos, their eyes wide with shock and confusion. "Disappear!" I bellow, a command laced with a threat that I hate to make. "Or else." I don't finish my threat.

Amira continues to fight against me. "I'm the best choice!" she insists, her voice cracking under the weight of her conviction. "You're wasting time, our time!" Her declaration is a plea, a demand, a vision of the future she's convinced herself of—one where competition and choice don't exist.

She lashes out again, catching me off guard for a second time. Her nails slice my skin once again, and I grip her arms, stopping her madness. Picking her up, I march down the stairs barefoot. She's still shouting.

"It should be just us." She's lost her fucking mind.

I don't stop until I reach the front door. I use one hand and open it, clearing the last steps until I deposit her onto the driveway.

"What are you doing?" She shouts as I turn and jog up the steps. I give her a stern look before I lock the door behind me. My face burns, and I touch my cheek. Fresh blood is sprinkled along my fingers.

I march up the stairs with a determination to find out what the fuck caused Niamh to freak out so badly.

CHAPTER TWENTY

AMIRA

RUINED... I'VE RUINED EVERYTHING. The realization hits me as I pick myself up from the concrete driveway, the cold seeping through the thin fabric of my dressing gown. I can't go home, yet the thought of fleeing to somewhere—anywhere—makes me realize I've nowhere else to go.

What have I done? Why did I lose my mind like that? Questions whirl in my head as the coldness of the driveway presses against my skin. My brain registers the chill, yet I can't bring myself to move, to react. I'm paralyzed, not just by the cold, but by the flood of memories and emotions that choose this moment to overwhelm me as I stare up at the mansion.

Dominic died this week, six years ago. I was just thirteen, barely stepping into my teenage years, when I lost my brother. My mother couldn't bear it. She couldn't bear most things, leaving me to grieve alone. Oh, God. How is she going to react to this news? The thought of facing her, of adding this failure to the mountain of disappointments that already defines our relationship, is unbearable.

I search the windows of all the rooms, trying to remember which one on the third floor we were in. Is Diarmuid up there with Selene and Niamh laughing at me? Did Niamh act like that for attention? Of course, she did; she was such a bitch to force my hand. Angry tears pour down my cheeks.

"Now, this is a view I rather enjoy." The words drip with unwelcome amusement and insinuation.

Wolf stands there in the driveway, his gaze not meeting my eyes but wandering in a manner that makes my skin crawl, focusing on parts of me as if I'm nothing more than an object for his viewing pleasure.

With Wolf's hungry gaze on me, I make no attempt to shield myself.

"I hoped I'd run into you again," he says, and the memory of watching him train the last girl assaults my memory, along with the things I learned watching him. I had used the same techniques on Diarmuid, hoping to gain the upper hand.

I don't speak, and Wolf takes a step closer.

"Speak to me." There is nothing soft in his words.

"I need to go home," is all I manage, my tone flat, devoid of the turmoil that rages inside me.

"Do you have Diarmuid's permission to leave?"

His question sparks a bitter smile that doesn't reach my eyes. "One could say that," I murmur, the irony not lost on me.

He looks at me for another minute. "I'll drop you home."

I don't exactly want to be alone with Wolf, but standing in the driveway with the image of Diarmuid and the girls laughing at me has me following him around the back of the mansion where his car waits.

The drive home is a silent journey, punctuated only by the occasional flick of Wolf's lighter and the soft exhale of smoke. The car's interior is filled with the sharp, acrid scent. Wolf doesn't fire any questions my way. Either he doesn't care, or his mind is somewhere else. It's a relief, in a way, to not have to explain, to not have to relive the humiliation and pain through recounting.

Outside, the city moves past us in a blur of lights and shadows. Streetlamps cast shadows on the pavement, fleeting glimpses of people living their lives—a couple laughing on a street corner, a group of friends sharing a late-night snack—moments of normalcy that seem so alien to me now. The world goes on, indifferent to the upheaval in my own life.

As we turn down the long driveway to my house, a sense of unreality washes over me. Wolf, without having asked, knew where to take me. Under different circumstances, I might have found that alarming, questioned how he knew where I lived. But tonight, I'm beyond caring, beyond questioning. I'm just a shell.

When the car comes to a stop, I don't thank Wolf. I don't say goodbye. I simply get out and walk toward my front door. Wolf is gone before I even close the door behind me.

The moment I step inside, the house embraces me with an eerie silence, save for the faint hum of light emanating from the kitchen. My body is a tight coil of tension as I tiptoe through the foyer. I want to go to my room, but the state of the entry to the kitchen stops me cold.

The trash can lies on its side, contents spilled. The sugar bowl, once a fixture on the counter, now lies shattered against the wall, its contents strewn about in a chaotic spray of white against the darkened tile. The scene is one of absolute destruction.

Despite my urge to keep moving, I'm rooted to the spot. And there, amid the devastation, sits my mother. Her presence is almost ghostly, her head resting on the countertop, her eyes closed.

For a suspended moment, I entertain the thought that she's finally drank herself to death. But then her eyes blink, and the harsh light of reality washes away the brief illusion of peace. Her face contorts.

"Amira!" Her scream sounds like a dying animal. It shatters the coldness inside me. I need to run to get to my room. But my legs won't cooperate.

"Get in here!" She roars again. I close my eyes briefly, praying for a respite from my mother's madness. If I don't do as she says, what will she do?

I take a small step into the chaos of the kitchen. I don't ask what happened.

When I come into full view, her face pinches in anger. "I would trade you for your brothers," she spits out, a confession so cruel it seems almost unholy. "I ask God every day to do this." Her words are venom, designed to wound, to break.

Her next words strike hard. "Whore," she hisses, a label meant to degrade, to diminish. It's a blow aimed not just at who I am but at the very essence of my being.

In that moment, something within me shifts. The pain of her words is real, but it ignites a spark of defiance. "You don't have to worry about me being a whore anymore," I respond, my voice steady despite the chaos inside. "I'm not a Bride anymore." It's a declaration, not just of my status but of my refusal to be caged by her judgments, her expectations.

"So, not only are you a whore, but you are a bad whore." Her voice drips with disdain.

My hands tighten into fists. "I am only a whore because you and Da fucked up our lives," I shoot back, my voice laced with a venom born of years of suppressed anger and hurt. "You're the reason why my virginity was given away. You're the reason why Da is out with the hooker of the week. You're the reason why my brothers are dead." I'm smiling as each word drips from my lips. I laugh at her as her face turns white.

She's still for a moment, but it's only a short moment before she launches herself from the seat, and my back slams heavily into the kitchen floor, taking the air from my lungs.

"You dirty bitch." She grabs the rubbish around us, stuffing it into my mouth, cutting off any air that tries to find its way into my starved lungs.

Before I can react, she drags me off the floor with a strength she shouldn't be able to wield. She turns the tap of the sink on, and cold water violently splashes across my face before she rams a bar of soap into my mouth.

"You will wash your mouth out, you sinful, sinful girl."

I choke on the acid taste of the soap. I push her away, and she stumbles, the soap dropping to the floor. She's ready to launch herself at me again when I scoop up ice-cold water and aim for her face. The shock has her screeching, but she's already grabbed a pan caked with grease and swings it, missing my face, but it slams against my shoulder. I cry out as I tumble to the ground.

"Get up!" she roars.

I'm stunned for a moment, but when her fingers curl around a cutting knife, I get to my feet. A sharp edge grazes my arm, drawing blood—a stark red line. The pain is sharp, and I try to wrestle the knife out of her hands. My bare foot slams down on her bare feet, and she cries in pain, her grip on the knife loosening. I scurry to the ground and pick it up, rising quickly to my feet and bringing the blade to her neck.

"You're a sorry excuse for a mother." Tears burn my face. My heart hammers in my chest. "I want you to die!!!" I roar into her face. "Die, you bitch." I scream again, pushing the blade. Something in me snaps as blood makes a trail down her neck. I drop the knife, the clang loud at our feet.

As I stagger away, the taste of blood coppery in my mouth and my wounds stinging painfully, I know that this is a turning point. I've lost everything. This is not just about survival; it's about forging a new path, one where my parents no longer dictate the direction of my future.

I take the first step up the stairs when a heavy weight lands on my back. I spin as my mother's fist connects with my jaw. She puts all her hate behind the thump, and I'm dazed for a moment. I shuffle up two more steps and spin, kicking her in the face. She falls down the three steps, and for a moment, her still frame makes a hysterical laugh bubble up my throat. But when she raises her head, I know she will kill me. I claw at the stairs, scrambling to get to the safety of my room.

"Get back here!" Her screams are right behind me.

Fear wraps its dark fingers around me as I dart through my bedroom door. My heart races, pounding against my chest with the same ferocity that my mother slams her body against the door just as I get it closed and turn the key. She pounds against my bedroom door. I can hear the wood complaining, threatening to give way under her relentless assault. If she gets in here, she will kill me. The thought flashes through my mind, clear and terrifying.

My jaw aches, and I'm dazed for a moment, but I scramble around my room. My eyes scan the familiar space for anything that might aid my escape.

Tennis shoes—I gather them up along with a sweater and a pair of jeans. I slip everything on in a heartbeat. Panic courses through me as another crash sounds at my door.

Next, cash. I hastily shoved it into my pocket from a drawer I'd always hoped would remain a secret. It's not much, but it's all I have.

The window is my only exit, and it looms in front of me like a beacon of hope. I wrench it open, the night air slapping my face, sobering me with its chill. I'm halfway through, one leg dangling out into the void, when the inevitable crash sounds behind me. The door has given in. My mother's fury has me scrambling, but I don't look back. I can't.

The fall from the window is brief, a momentary flight that ends with my feet hitting the ground hard. I stumble, but I don't fall. Adrenaline is a miraculous thing, lending me the strength and speed I didn't know I possessed. As I run, my mother's rage-filled screams chase me, a haunting soundtrack that follows behind long after I've escaped into the night.

But for now, I run. I run from a house that was never a home, from a woman who was never truly a mother. Each step is an alchemy of liberation and terror. The night is cold as I race away from my mother and into the unknown.

CHAPTER TWENTY-ONE

NIAMH

I'M NESTLED HALFWAY BETWEEN the stage and the back doors of the Gaiety Theater. To my left is my mother, her attention riveted upon the unfolding spectacle. My father occupies the space on her other side. Both are engrossed, their gazes never straying from the stage. Around us, a sea of formally dressed spectators share in this silent performance.

The dancers, with their vibrant costumes and energetic movements, bring the story of the four seasons to life. Winter's chill has been banished, making way for Spring's vivacity. It's a transformation I've witnessed year after year, yet it never ceases to stir something within me. The stage is awash with colors.

I search for one performer among the many. Ella, my sister, the one person I can pinpoint in a crowd of a million without fail. Tonight, though, her role makes her stand out even more. Not a flower, nor a bird. No,

Ella is Bacchante—a character with a name, a story, a presence that is undeniably her own.

A swell of pride rises in me. She embodies Bacchante with such conviction that, for a moment, I forget she's playing a role. To me, she's the very essence of Spring itself—wild, joyful, and unrestrained.

Intermission breaks the enchantment of the performance with the stark reality of a crowded space. The stage, just moments ago alive with the vivid storytelling of dancers, now lies hidden behind the heavy curtains, awaiting the second act. Dancers in yellow cloaks mark the transition, their movements a whirlwind of color and grace, guiding their fellow performers offstage in a final, fleeting tableau before the curtains draw close.

The shift in the auditorium is immediate. A collective exhale fills the air, the sound of hundreds of people rising, stretching limbs stiffened by the long sit, engaging in whispered conversations, or navigating the aisles toward the restrooms or concession stands.

I watch as my parents stand, my father taking the lead as he always does from his preferred spot at the end of the row. They merge into the stream of people, my mother's voice barely audible over the hum of the crowd, discussing Ella's performance—every movement, every leap, every turn scrutinized. The pride in her achievement is tempered by a relentless pursuit of perfection. Even in this moment of triumph, the conversation centers on what could be better, on the imperfections only a trained eye could catch. It's an all-too-familiar pattern, their high expectations always casting a long shadow.

I find myself alone, my parents' attention anchored to Ella's performance. Their absence by my side is a familiar scenario on nights like these, where my sister's talent steals all their attention. Oddly enough, I like this time alone.

Navigating the throng of intermission-goers, I push my way out of the theater and onto the sidewalk. The transition from the artificially lit interior to the outside world is startling. The grand arc of the theater's entrance frames my exit as I step into the crisp embrace of the autumn air. The freshness of it is nice after the warmth of the theater and the intoxicating scents of perfumes and aftershaves.

Outside, the city is alive—the distant hum of traffic blends with the closer sounds of conversations and footsteps on pavement. Streetlights cast a golden glow.

My moment of solitude is cut short by an usher who approaches me as I attempt to re-enter the theater for the second act.

"Niamh Connolly?" He asks, an odd formality in his tone.

"Yes."

He nods. "I am here to lead you back to your seat." He holds out his arm for me to go ahead.

"I already know where my seat is," I say.

"Let me have the honor." He smiles softly.

As I follow the usher up the stairs and down a hallway tinged with the muffled sounds of an audience settling back into their seats, a familiar anticipation builds within me. The red curtains that mark the entrance to the private boxes loom ahead, but it's the sight of one particular box, distinguished by its door, that signals this is no ordinary seating upgrade.

The usher opens the door, and I peek inside. Diarmuid is there, his presence commanding even in his silence.

"Sit next to me," he says without even turning around.

The opulence of the private box is immediately apparent, not just in its furnishings but also in the presence of bodyguards, discreetly hidden behind curtains at both the front and back.

"Leave us." Diarmuid's terse command has them departing, and it leaves us alone.

As I take my seat beside him, my attention is involuntarily drawn to Diarmuid. Dressed for the occasion, his appearance transcends the usual definitions of formal attire. There's an undeniable elegance to him, a refinement that accentuates his presence. The realization that he's both familiar and entirely enigmatic brings a blush to my cheeks. Here is a man who has changed the course of my life, and yet, the gravity of our situation feels all the more real in this secluded setting.

Selene's warnings echo in my mind that Diarmuid is dangerous. That he survives, and indeed, thrives in his world is a testament to his strength and perhaps, to aspects of his character that are better left unexplored. The severity of his deeds, as hinted by Selene, keeps rising to the forefront of my mind.

As the curtains of the box draw back and the performance resumes with the vibrant depiction of Summer, Diarmuid breaks the silence. His voice is calm amidst the storm of my thoughts.

"I wanted to make sure you are okay after the other night," he starts.

My body tenses at that question. The night he put his hands around my neck, and all I could think about was that poor girl in the morgue, with marks around her neck, too. I don't think Diarmuid killed her, but it had pulled me under a dark current of fear and panic that I wasn't able to escape that night, not even when he had returned and questioned me. I had no answer for him then, and I have none I can give him now.

"You're kind," I say, a simple truth.

"You are one of my Brides, a role that carries with it duties and responsibilities. It's my job to take care of you," he answers simply.

"What about Amira?" I ask, remembering she hadn't returned after he had escorted her from the room.

"Amira is my concern, not yours."

Maybe he's right. I'm not overly fond of her. I take another peek at Diarmuid. "How did you know I was here, and how did you get tickets?"

He looks at me, and a slow smile crosses his lips.

"The Kings own the private box," he states.

This doesn't surprise me as much as it should. Their reach and influence, it seems, extend even into the cultural heart of the city.

"And how I knew where you were… I had you followed." He continues with a matter-of-fact tone.

However, the fact that Diarmuid had me followed here sends a chill down my spine. It's one thing to be under the protective gaze of a powerful organization, quite another to be shadowed without my knowledge.

"Why am I being followed?"

Diarmuid doesn't answer straightaway, as if he is weighing his words. "The organization has its own unseen dangers; this level of protection and surveillance is necessary."

That doesn't exactly answer my question. His lack of detail shows me he doesn't fully trust me. But we don't know each other that well. The only time we are together is with Selene and Amira.

"Why are you here, at this ballet?" he asks, shifting the conversation. I allow the turn of questioning, knowing I'm not going to get any more out of him.

"My sister Ella is in the play. She has the role of Bacchante. She's only sixteen, so her role is very significant for someone her age. "

"It sounds like your sister has a bright future ahead of her," he states.

"I guess."

"The role of Bacchante at sixteen doesn't guarantee success in the world of ballet?"

The moment stretches between us, charged with an energy I can't quite name. Diarmuid's gaze is intent, probing, as if he's trying to read the very essence of my thoughts. It's disconcerting, and yet, I find myself unable to look away.

"Well, the first woman to play Bacchante, Marie Petipa, ended up dying of impulsive insanity," I share, a bit of trivia slipping out in an attempt to lighten the mood or maybe to impress him with my knowledge.

He chuckles dryly, the sound echoing slightly in the spacious box. "You must be a very supportive sister to know so much about ballet."

The comment stings, though I know he doesn't mean it to. I shift uncomfortably in my seat. "This used to be my world," I confess, a hint of nostalgia coloring my words.

"You hated it," Diarmuid observes, more a statement than a question.

I nod, the admission slipping out easier than I expected. "I did. But my mother... She wants a prima ballerina in the family."

"Your sister isn't a prima ballerina now?" he probes, his interest piqued.

"No, to be a prima ballerina, Ella needs to be accepted into a major ballet company and then become the best dancer in that company," I explain, my voice tinged with a mix of hope and realism.

"So, it's like being a general," Diarmuid muses.

"Or a King," I add, my words a bridge between our worlds.

The conversation shifts subtly, Diarmuid's gaze intensifying. "And you? What do you want to do with your life?"

I take a deep breath, my own dream suddenly feeling small and insignificant in the grandeur of this setting. "I want to conquer the Oceans Seven. To be a professional swimmer."

Diarmuid's response is noncommittal, a simple nod that prompts me to push further. "What about you? What's your dream?"

"When you don't really own your life, what use are dreams?" His words are a whisper, heavy with a resignation that surprises me.

The question hangs in the air, unanswered, as the ballet resumes onstage.

The rest of the show unfolds in a shared silence that feels both comfortable and charged with unspoken thoughts. For a moment, the world outside this private box, with its dangers and complexities, fades away. I'm just Niamh, Ella's sister, lost in the beauty of the ballet.

As Ella takes her final bow, something within me ignites. I forget about the formalities, the presence of Diarmuid, the weight of his world pressing in on us. Rising to my feet, I applaud with abandon, my hands coming together in a loud, fervent praise for my sister's performance. In this moment, I am every inch the proud sister, my heart swelling with pride.

As the curtain falls for the last time and the audience begins to filter out, the reality of my surroundings—and my company—settles back in. I'm still standing when I turn to Diarmuid. "Thank you," I say, sincere in my gratitude for the experience, for the view, for the momentary escape from my parents, who I bet haven't even wondered where I am.

He gestures for me to wait, moving with a deliberate calm to close the outer curtains of our box, sealing us away from the departing crowd. The privacy feels suddenly intimate, a world apart from the grand spectacle we've just witnessed.

Then, he turns to me, the intensity in his eyes a stark contrast to the quiet endearment of earlier conversations. "I want to know exactly how you like to be touched, what you want from me," he says, his voice low and earnest. "I've been restless since our last encounter, and I want to make it right."

His words hang between us: a confession, a question, a plea. It's a moment of vulnerability, of honesty, that strips away the layers of his guarded existence. In this secluded box, away from the prying eyes of the world, Diarmuid is not a figure shrouded in mystery and power but a man seeking connection, seeking understanding.

The air shifts around us, filled with a new tension, a new possibility. As I meet his gaze, a thousand thoughts race through my mind, each one a reflection of my own uncertainties, desires, and fears. Yet, beneath it all, there's a flicker of something else—curiosity, perhaps, or even the thrill of stepping into unknown territory.

In this moment, the roles we play—the King and his Bride, the protector and the protected—seem to fade, leaving us simply as Diarmuid and Niamh.

"I'm not sure." My voice rattles.

Diarmuid nods and clears the distance between us. "If I did this, would it be okay?" He takes my face gently in his hands and presses a soft kiss to my lips. I taste mint, it's refreshing, and when he sinks his tongue into my mouth, I press mine into his.

The buzz of the voices of hundreds of people below us sounds distant. The lighting in the private box is dim as Diarmuid breaks the kiss and smiles down at me. Being around Diarmuid before, I've always been shy, but having him alone, changes something in me. I reach up and press my lips to his.

The invitation unleashes a desire in him that surprises me; his kisses are hungry, and his hand warms around my waist, pulling me closer to him. I can feel the full extent of his excitement. My own dampen between my thighs.

A thought assaults me as fast as the strike of lightning. *I like having him to myself.*

I want to be as bold as Amira and as courageous as Selene. I let my hand slip across his wide chest and move lower and lower until I touch him. The outline of his bulge feels huge against my hands. He had almost taken my virginity the other night, but the act wasn't complete. The idea of having him take it with just the two of us present makes me grip him harder and rub his full length. He groans into my mouth, his minty breath filling my own.

He breaks the kiss and rests his forehead against mine. He's still as I continue to rub his full length. His eyes are closed, but he groans in pleasure.

After a moment, he opens his eyes, and his hand leaves my waist and trails down further, where he bunches up the fabric of my dark red dress, gathering it slowly. The cool air touches my bare legs, and anticipation has me frozen for a moment.

"Is this okay?" he asks as his fingers touch my bare skin.

I nod.

He continues until he touches my panties, damp with a need that both shocks me and has me leaning in closer to his hand.

"Can I taste you?"

I glance at the balcony that gave us a view of the stage. It's now blocked with the red, heavy drapes. People still talk below us, but I know no one can see.

I nod again.

Diarmuid sits back down in my chair and pulls up my dress. He's kneeling at my feet, his gaze fixed on my face for a moment before he bends over. Pulling my panties aside, he gives his tongue access to my folds and parts them.

I hiss with pure pleasure. He's done this before, but being alone makes it feel different, more intimate.

He laps at my folds, and my body threatens to re-lease the build-up that's quickly gathering inside me, but Diarmuid's licking turns to kisses that he continues pressing the whole way down my leg. Each kiss feels like he's branding ownership into my flesh. He lifts my leg and slips off my high heel. He watches me as he places kisses along the inside of my foot.

"What do you want, Niamh?" His voice is husky with his own desire.

I know what I want. I'm just not sure I'm brave enough to say it, but as I glance around the dimly lit box, I know it's now or never.

"I want you to take me," I say.

He nods and rises to his feet, holding out his hands. I take them as he pulls me to my feet. He spins me and pulls me into his chest. Kisses are placed along my neck, and the sound of the crowd below turns to a soft buzz as I'm consumed by his roaming hands across my torso and the kisses he continues to place along my neck. He gathers the fabric of my dress again until he's holding it securely around my waist. His lips touch my ear. "Hold onto the chair and bend over," he whispers and kisses my ear again.

I grip the velvet of the back of the chair and arch my ass into him. I take over, holding up my dress. Warmth rushes to my checks as I hear his zipper, belt, and then the shuffle of the material of his trousers.

His fingers prod between my legs, and my eyes flutter closed at the contact. It's only for a moment before he removes them, and a larger, meatier body part is placed at my opening. He pushes himself into me slowly, stretching me, filling me up. It burns slightly, just like the last time. One hand grips my hip while the other runs up and down my spine in a soothing movement, and then he withdraws slightly before pushing into me again. This time, the burn is less. My core squeezes around his cock, and I find myself pushing further into him.

"You are perfect," he whispers. His voice sounds strained, like he's struggling to hold this steady flow of in and out. He's being careful with me, knowing I'm a virgin, and that makes my stomach tighten with appreciation and need.

He moves inside me again and pulls out; he keeps this steady rhythm as he runs his fingers up and down my spine.

I keep my hold on my dress that's gripping the chair, and with my other hand, I reach down and touch my clit. The contact sends a new thrill through me, and I gasp as more sensations seem to override everything else.

I don't know how he senses my need, but he starts to move faster, in and out of me. I'm so close to coming my body screams for release. I turn just enough to meet Diarmuid's gaze. I don't know what he sees, but he starts to move faster, and I turn back, working my clit. The climax is like the final scene of the ballet, and I'm falling, calling out as the lights shatter behind my eyes, and I come fast and hard.

When I open my eyes, I'm panting, a light sprinkle of sweat on my forehead.

"Oh, fuck." I manage to say between dry lips.

A half-snort laugh from Diarmuid, has me apologizing.

"Please don't apologize," he says, removing himself from me and fixes my dress into place. I take a moment to gather some courage to face him, and when I stand straight, Diarmuid is dressed and holding my shoe in his hand.

He smiles happily at me as he kneels down and helps me place my foot into the shoe. It's a real Cinderella moment as my prince rises.

"Did you…" I trail off, I'm wondering if he came.

"No," he confesses and takes my face in his hands. "But we will have plenty of time for that."

I nod, slightly disappointed.

"It was perfect." His kind words chase my worries away.

"I'd better get back to my parents. I'm sure they are wondering where I got to." It's a half-truth; I doubt they even noticed my disappearance.

But Diarmuid places a kiss on my forehead. "Okay."

I'm flustered as I enter the lobby. My parents stand together, with no sign of Ella. She will be with the production crew celebrating tonight.

My mother is the first to spot me. I blush, but she doesn't seem to notice.

"Where were you? I want to get home," she says.

I scramble to find an answer.

But she's so caught up in her own thoughts that she waves me off. "The car is here, let's go."

I follow my parents out of the theater and take one final look at the milling crowd in the lobby, but I don't see Diarmuid. I hope I won't have to wait long to see him again.

CHAPTER TWENTY-TWO

DIARMUID

I'M DRIVING HOME; THE night air is cool against my skin, and my mind is a tumultuous sea. The last remnants of Niamh's taste linger on my lips, and unconsciously, my fingers trace them, seeking more of her, more of that sweet, intoxicating essence. The streets are nearly empty, lit by the occasional streetlamp.

Three women. Each one is so different.

Amira. Her mistake was a crack in the otherwise impeccable facade she presented to the world. But who among us is without fault? My hope by placing her on the driveway the other night was to let her cool down. I need to go check on her and see if she has, in fact, calmed down.

Then there's Selene. Fierce doesn't even begin to cover it. She's a fortress with walls I've been trying to scale since the moment we met. Her resistance only fuels my desire, turning every encounter into a battle of wills I'm determined to win. There's something about the chase, the constant push and pull, that's exhilarating.

And Niamh. Sweet, delicate Niamh. Every moment with her is a tightrope walk between joy and despair. She's fragile, not in body but in spirit, and I fear the world I inhabit will shatter her. She deserves so much more, and I'm caught between wanting to give her everything and fearing that I'll be her undoing.

The ring of my cell phone cuts through my reverie like a knife. It's one of my men. "Boss, we've got a problem. The shipment's delayed."

Right, the business. My life isn't just consumed right now by my Brides; there's the ever-present weight of my empire. Between juggling alliances and unearthing traitors, I've had to lean heavily on my crew. The O'Sullivan arms trade doesn't run itself, after all.

"There's more," he hesitates, and in that pause, a cold shiver runs down my spine. I hear a murmur in the background, a voice that shouldn't be there. A voice I know.

Wolf.

I grip the steering wheel tighter, the leather groaning under my fingers. Wolf's presence is never a harbinger of good news. He's the shadow in my already dark world, a reminder that there are always bigger predators lurking, waiting.

The turn of my wheel toward the Dublin Docklands is a decisive one, pulling me away from any lingering thoughts of checking in on Amira. Priorities constantly shift in my line of work, and the call involving Wolf demands immediate attention. The road stretches before me, leading to a place that blends day-to-day commerce with the undercurrents of a world unseen by most.

The Dublin Docklands, with its bustling activity and scenic views, is a veneer of normalcy and tourism. It's almost laughable how one of the country's vital arteries, handling the lion's share of Ireland's imports and exports, doubles as a stage for criminal enterprises. Tourists flock here, oblivious to the underbelly, drawn by the promise of leisure and the charm of waterside eateries and sporting events. They wander, dine, and celebrate, all under the watchful gaze of cranes that toil in the distance.

I pull into a private space beside The Silent Prince Tavern, a pub that's mastered the art of camouflage.

Its exterior is a careful construction designed to appeal to tourists with its quaint charm and the allure of an old-world tavern. The sign swaying gently in the night breeze—a young prince, crowned and commanding silence with a finger pressed to his lips—is a fitting emblem for the secrets it guards.

Inside, the atmosphere is rich in Irish culture. The air is alive with the strum of folk music, a melody that's both balm and a blade, cutting through my thoughts. Around me, tourists and locals laugh and chatter. Televisions flicker with the vibrant greens of the Croke Park football field.

Alan, the head bartender, catches my eye from across the room. He signals to one of the bartenders and begins to make his way over. His approach is a casual saunter. No one gives us a second glance as we move together toward the back of the pub, the world of drinks and banter falling away with each step.

The door to the back office closes with a soft click, sealing us away from the lively pulse of the pub.

The office gives way to a hidden world behind a false wall. The sound of hissing kegs filters through as the front continues its normal operation of serving drinks. Inside, the air is cooler, filled with the scent of wood, and a quiet tension seems to fill the room. Organized crates line the walls while a group of men stand huddled around a table in the center.

Without hesitation, I address the matter at hand, my voice cutting through the murmur of conversation. "Where's Wolf?"

"He just left before you arrived," Alan says with a frown, like my line of questioning shouldn't matter.

One of my men steps forward, worry clear in his expression. "The ship was supposed to have our order, but it arrived empty. Clients are waiting, Diarmuid."

I approach the table, poring over the logs laid out before me. Two possibilities unfold in my mind: either our contacts faced unexpected trouble, redirecting our cargo to one of two alternate ships, or our shipment has been intercepted and stolen or discovered. Neither scenario bodes well for us.

"Who's on this?" I ask Alan.

His response, a single name, Fergal, does little to quell the churn of thoughts in my mind. "Is Fergal up to this?" I press.

Alan's nod is firm. "He's earned his stripes, Diarmuid. Been through the fire with us."

"Where was the shipment coming from?" I ask.

"Russia."

The thought of Russia tightens the coil of tension in my gut. International complications are the last thing we need.

As we agree to wait for word from Fergal, Alan pulls me aside, his voice low. "Should we get the others involved?" he whispers.

"The others?" I question.

"Yeah, you know, the others." Alan raises both brows.

I know he's referring to the Hand of Kings. The O'Sullivans have navigated treacherous waters before without needing the Hand of Kings' help. "The O'Sullivans have been handling shit like this for centuries," I assert firmly. "We just need to know what screw needs twisting. Get on that." My voice leaves no room for argument.

As I step back into the lively atmosphere of the bar, the familiar sights and sounds wrap around me like a cloak. In another life, or perhaps just a different chapter of my own, I would have melted into this scene with ease. The counter, the clink of glasses, the hum of conversation—a backdrop against which I'd play out the night's possibilities. The apartments above, silent witnesses to countless nights where I've brought women to fuck. Yet, tonight, that doesn't interest me.

Maybe I am starting to feel something for one of my Brides. With that thought, I find myself at the counter, not to find a woman to fuck, but to seek the simple comfort of whiskey. The bartender places a white napkin in front of me before placing a freshly poured whiskey on top of it. The amber liquid holds a promise of temporary respite, a fleeting escape.

As I lift the glass, the presence of another at my elbow pulls me back to the present. Wolf. His appearance is both unexpected and not. He apparently didn't go too far.

"Why are you here?" I ask and bring the drink to my lips. I take a sip.

"I'm an O'Sullivan, too. There is no reason why I can't be here. It's part of my family's history."

I drink half the glass before turning to Wolf.

"Bullshit," I call out. I wasn't born yesterday.

"Fine." Wolf shrugs. "I was looking for you. I'm going stir crazy since our meeting with Victor." Wolf speaks too loudly but I don't get to scold him as he turns to the bartender and raises two fingers, beckoning him forward.

"You have to sit tight," I say and finish my drink. Staying here with Wolf isn't something I want to do.

"Get me a whiskey," Wolf orders the bartender, who looks at me. I shake my head letting him know I don't want any more.

"How is Amira?" Wolf asks.

The mention of Amira, said so casually from Wolf's lips, ignites a fury within me that's hard to contain. "Why the hell are you interested in her?" My question is a demand.

"Relax, Diarmuid. I've just got something for her." His words, meant to diffuse, only fan the flames. The notion that Amira might need something from him, that there's a connection there I'm unaware of, is intolerable. "Anything she needs can go through me," I assert, a line drawn in the sand.

"I'm afraid that this isn't something that can simply be handed over, Diarmuid," He picks up his drink and takes a swallow.

Who the fuck does he think he is? I take a step toward him, thinking I could break him like I broke his father. Would he scream and plead as loud as his father? I'm sure Wolf would cry and offer up anything or anyone just to save his skin. My hands reach out and grab Wolf by the collar of his jacket. His brows shoot up as if he's surprised that I'm pissed.

Alan appears on the far side of Wolf, and he is the only thing that prevents me from hurting Wolf. A nod from me has Alan stepping back. I can control myself. I release Wolf, but he doesn't appear to be relieved that I didn't hurt him. His eyes tighten in anger.

"You are always protected, watched over." A bitterness enters Wolf's voice as he watches Alan walk away, and when Wolf turns back to me, he gives a laugh. "Of course, I can't touch Diarmuid O'Sullivan. Not in his own place."

Is he fucking mocking me?

"Lorcan is protected by his political circle. Ronan is protected by the thugs he can hire through his business contacts." Angry words roll from his tongue before he comes to the punchline.

"It's obvious Victor is planning to cut me out of my inheritance."

I find myself momentarily at a loss for words. The O'Sullivan family, my family, is indeed a well-oiled machine, each cog turning in unison even amidst the turmoil of our patriarch's decline. Victor's silence on the matter of succession has left us in a state of suspended anticipation, each of us awaiting his signal to align ourselves accordingly.

The right to choose our leader, once held firmly within our grasp, was relinquished the moment we entwined our fate with the Hand of Kings. A decision that, while expanding our reach and solidifying our power, also bound us to their will, making the succession a matter of their interest as much as ours.

Wolf, as a leader, is a thought I can barely entertain. His temperand his darkness make him unsuitable for a role that demands not just strength but restraint. Our world, as unforgiving as it is, requires a leader who can navigate its shadows without being consumed by them. Wolf's love for breaking things wouldn't bode well for him.

"My father was going to give me everything. I was going to take over."

This is a complete surprise to me. I know I should say I'm sorry, but the words would sound as empty as they are.

"Do you remember where you were that night, the night Andrew disappeared?"

The bartender arrives back, and I'm so grateful for the distraction. "I'll have another." I turn to Wolf, but his drink is still full.

"I was probably in the pub, managing my affairs," I respond with a nonchalance I don't quite feel. The question, pointed as it is, dredges up memories better left undisturbed.

"This man was your uncle," he presses, an edge of accusation in his tone. "I know exactly where I was and what I was doing that night. Why can't you remember?"

"I'm a busy man," I counter, the defense sounding feeble even to my own ears.

"We were all at the Church for drinks. Lorcan and Ronan were in town, everyone was there... except you." Wolf has never sounded so sure about anything in his life.

The world around us grows silent, and I know I better get my head straight, quickly.

"If I wasn't there, then I would have been at The Silent Prince," I offer and reach for my drink.

He nods, a gesture heavy with unspoken implications. "Lorcan called Alan that night. Alan said you weren't at the pub, either."

The silence that follows is charged, a tangible thing that stretches between us, laden with questions and accusations unvoiced. I look into Wolf's eyes, seeing not just my cousin but the memories of a shared past. Wolf knows me, perhaps better than anyone—my preferences, my weaknesses, my secrets, well, not all my secrets. A formidable ally, indeed, but in another life, perhaps an even more formidable foe.

Wolf nods, like he got an answer, before he reaches across and picks up my drink.

He drinks the entire glass in one swallow and walks away.

CHAPTER
TWENTY-THREE
SELENE

T HE AIR IS BRISK and carries with it the scent of city life—coffee, the faint hint of exhaust, and the promise of rain. Grafton Street buzzes around us, alive and vibrant. I'm walking alongside Niamh, her presence a comforting constant in the pulsating heart of the city. The shops gleam with the allure of luxury, their windows filled with colors and lights, but it's the simple joy of exploration with Niamh that I find myself cherishing the most.

We come to a halt before a statue, its bronze form a tribute to a woman whose story is woven into the fabric of Dublin's history. The statue depicts her with corsets that daringly reveal the top part of her breasts, a silent yet bold testament to her existence—or the lack thereof, depending on who you ask.

"People say she never really existed," I muse aloud, tracing the lines of the statue with my eyes.

Niamh looks at me, her brows furrowing slightly. "That's ridiculous. How can they say Mary Malone was just...made up?"

I lean closer, dropping my voice to a conspiratorial whisper. "There was a mix-up with the record-keeping. Turns out, Mary Malone wasn't exactly who everyone thought she was."

Niamh's gaze drifts to the statue, to the baskets in the wheelbarrow, empty.

"That's probably why she had to sell herself," I say softly with humor.

Niamh laughs softly and links her arm with mine as we resume walking.

"I think she was real." Niamh declares as we walk along the repaved street.

The murmur of conversations envelops us. "What are you craving to eat?" I ask.

Niamh's response is hesitant, tinged with vulnerability. "I'm still getting used to not counting calories or carbohydrates in my food. Being an athlete...it did a number on how I see food."

I squeeze her arm gently, a silent vow forming between us. "We'll fix that. First, we go for Chinese. Then, when we're ready for round two, we'll hit the chocolate store."

Niamh looks at me, surprise etched on her face.

"An entire store dedicated to chocolate. It will be glorious," I grip her hand for a moment with excitement.

As we continue our stroll, a thought bubbles to the surface. "I once dreamed of opening a store here," I confess, the words slipping out before I can weigh their impact.

Niamh's interest is piqued, her eyes lighting up with curiosity. "Oh? What kind of store? A bookstore?"

The guess brings a smile to my face. "You would think, but no. I wanted to open an amezaiku store.

"Amezaiku?" She echoes, her expression a blend of confusion and intrigue.

"It's a very artistic style of Japanese candy making," I explain, the memories of my fascination unfurling like the pages of a well-loved book. "I was obsessed with it for about two years. It was one of those dreams that shine brightly for a moment before fading into the backdrop of reality."

Niamh's interest seems to deepen. "You had other dreams?"

"Too many," I admit with a laugh, a sound that feels both free and a little sad. "My parents let me explore anything that caught my fancy."

"That sounds nice," she muses, a note of wistfulness in her voice.

"It was, in its own way. But in the end, we both ended up in the same place, didn't we?" I say, a subtle acknowledgment of our shared journey, of paths that diverged and converged in the most unexpected of ways.

Our conversation shifts to lighter topics as we secure some Chinese takeout, the warmth of the containers promising comfort and satiation. However, our search for a bench to enjoy our meal proves fruitless; every potential spot is already claimed, a testament to the city's bustle and life.

Undeterred, I lead us to a quiet piece of wall on the side of a building, an improvised spot that offers respite and a view of the street's vibrant dance. Sitting down, I lean my back against the cool brick, feeling its solid presence grounding me. Niamh joins me, her own back finding the wall, and we sit side by side in companionable silence, the city's hum a backdrop to our shared meal.

The rice is divine, with just the right amount of honey sauce poured on, and I find small cuttings of filet beef mixed like prizes amongst the rice and peppers.

"So, what happened at the theater?" I ask. I had tried to ask earlier, but Niamh had avoided my question. She was so obvious; now I need to know what took place.

Niamh's cheeks color with a sudden blush, her eyes darting away, and I can't help but smile at her bashfulness. "Why are you blushing?" I tease, trying to ease her discomfort. "You're a grown woman, and there's nothing to be ashamed of. And, if you're worried about someone overhearing, there's no one close enough to care. Even if they did, no one knows us, anyway."

She hesitates, then, looking at me with a mix of admiration and incredulity, she changes the subject. "How can you think about shopping, food, and... other things when there's so much bad happening in the world?"

Her question strikes a chord deep within me, a reminder of a truth I seldom visit. I recall the moment my
parents revealed the nature of my existence to them—not
as a daughter cherished and loved for who she is but
as a commodity, a pawn in their social maneuverings.
I had idolized them, believing in their affection and
support, only to discover their warmth was as hollow as
the echoes in a deserted hall. The realization had come
crashing down on me during a stay at my grandparents'
where the absence of genuine love in my upbringing
became painfully clear.

Yet, this revelation, this understanding of my place
in my family's world, is not something I wish to lay
upon Niamh's shoulders. So, I choose simplicity over the
weight of my history. "If you worry about something
that's going to happen, you suffer twice," I say, hoping
to offer a sliver of wisdom amidst the uncertainty.

Niamh pauses, considering my words. "Buddhism?"
she ventures, a hint of a smile tugging at her lips.

"Close!" I laugh, shaking my head at Niamh's guess.
"Seneca, a Roman philosopher."

Niamh rolls her eyes playfully, and for a moment,
the tension between us eases. We're just two friends

sharing lunch, not competitors in a bizarre contest for love. But even as we banter, my mind drifts to Diarmuid—charismatic, enigmatic Diarmuid. It's easy to get lost in discussions about his many fine qualities; his charm is undeniable, his smile infectious. But beneath the surface, there's a darkness that nags at me, a shadow I can't ignore.

"He's got this... aura, doesn't he?" Niamh muses, her voice tinged with a mix of admiration and curiosity.

I nod, trying to focus on the conversation, but my thoughts betray me, wandering to that haunting image. Diarmuid, a man capable of killing without hesitation. The rumor of him killing a child whispers in my mind, a sinister lullaby that won't let me rest. I glance at Niamh, wondering if I should share my fears. But what if knowing puts her in danger? What if ignorance is her shield?

We drift to lighter topics, like Diarmuid's peculiar habit of always keeping his shirt on. "Maybe he's hiding a tattoo," Niamh suggests, her eyes sparkling with mischief.

"Or maybe scars from some secret past," I add, trying to match her levity. We weave theories as fantastical as the tales of old, each more absurd than the last. But the laughter doesn't reach my eyes, and I wonder if Niamh notices.

Lunch ends, and we dispose of our garbage, the mundane act grounding me for a moment. As we link arms, heading towards the chocolate store, I can't help but marvel at the strangeness of our situation. Here we are, acting like lifelong friends, yet we're rivals, each hoping to win Diarmuid's heart. I think of Amira and the last time we saw her.

"Have you heard from Amira lately?" I ask, the question slipping out before I can stop it.

Niamh's expression sours slightly. "I try not to talk to her even when we're in the same room," she admits, and there's a bitterness in her voice that surprises me.

As I lean over the counter, watching the chocolatier package our order with an artisanal touch, Niamh's phone shatters the cozy atmosphere of the shop. She steps aside, her expression shifting from casual curiosity to intense focus. I try to distract myself with the array of chocolates, but the undercurrent of our situation tugs at me, pulling me back to a reality I'd rather forget.

When Niamh ends the call, her eyes meet mine, holding a storm within them. "It was Rian," she says, her voice a mix of hope and dread. "He thinks he has the identity of the woman."

A chill runs down my spine, and the delicious aromas around me suddenly don't register. The weight of our investigation crashes into me with renewed force. We're not just playing a game of affection and intrigue; we're knee-deep in a conspiracy, a murder. The realization makes my earlier worries seem naive, a fool's errand of trying to compartmentalize my life into manageable, unthreatening pieces.

I watch as the last of the chocolates are tucked into the box, the ribbon tied with a flourish that now feels grotesquely out of place. Turning to Niamh, I muster a faint smile; the question about the chocolate feels hollow. "Do you... want your chocolate?" My voice is barely above a whisper, laced with a sudden lack of appetite that mirrors my inner turmoil.

Niamh shakes her head, her gaze distant. "Not hungry," she murmurs, and I can see the gears turning behind her eyes, processing the call with Rian, the implications of what he's discovered.

We leave the shop, the box of chocolates in my hand feeling like a leaden weight. Neither of us has the heart to indulge in them, not with the shadow of the murder looming over us. As we walk, the streets seem less vibrant, the laughter and chatter around us a discordant soundtrack to the grim reality we're entangled in. The sweet anticipation of enjoying our treats evaporates, replaced by a cold determination to face whatever comes next.

Rian's apartment feels like a storm's epicenter as we step inside. He dashes back to his cluttered table in a whirlwind of papers without a word of greeting. His excitement is palpable, infectious even, but I'm rooted to the spot, a sense of dread building within me.

"It wasn't easy," Rian starts, his words tumbling out as fast as he moves, shuffling through the documents with frenzied precision. "I've been at this non-stop since you described the composite sketch. And you won't believe where I finally found her identity—a paparazzi blog, of all places."

Niamh and I exchange a look. The absurdity of the situation is not lost on us, yet the gravity of what Rian says anchors us to the moment. He slides a photograph across the table toward us, his fingers trembling slightly with the weight of his discovery.

The woman in the photo turns, her gaze caught by the camera as if she knew this moment was coming. She's beautiful, undeniably so, with an elegance that seems at odds with her fate. Her hair, styled perfectly, frames her face, and the black dress under her peacoat speaks of a night out, perhaps one filled with laughter and life—so starkly different from how her story ended.

Looking at her, alive and vibrant, sends a chill through me, a visceral reaction as the memory of the bruising around her neck flashes in my mind. It's a stark reminder of the brutality she faced, a contrast so jarring against the glamorous image before us. My stomach turns, the injustice of her death a heavy, suffocating blanket.

"She looks..." Niamh starts, her voice trailing off, lost in the same morass of emotions that I'm drowning in.

"Like she didn't deserve what happened to her," I finish for her, my voice barely a whisper. The room feels smaller somehow, the walls closing in as the reality of what we're dealing with settles heavily on my shoulders. We're not just hunting shadows; we're seeking justice for a woman who had her life cruelly snatched away.

"Her name is Sofia Hughes," Rian announces, the solemnity in his tone contrasting sharply with his earlier excitement. My gaze shifts back to the photo, to Sofia's image, and I don't doubt him for a second. The resemblance to the body we saw, to the sketch the coroner had, is undeniable. The article he's referring to paints a picture of a woman caught in a dangerous liaison—a freelance journalist rumored to be entangled with someone high up in the government.

"A cover-up for an affair," I murmur, the words tasting bitter on my tongue. "But murder... It seems so drastic."

Niamh is quiet for a moment; her thoughts are obviously elsewhere. Then, hesitantly, she asks, "Is Sofia's family looking for her?" Her voice is tinged with a personal anguish that doesn't escape me. I know she's thinking of her own sister, the fear of something happening to her lurking in the back of her mind.

Rian doesn't miss a beat, pulling up a social media post on his laptop. It's a plea from Sofia's sister, Nessa, asking about Sofia's whereabouts. The post is accompanied by a photo of Sofia and Nessa together, laughing as they share ice cream. Their joy is palpable, their smiles bright, yet now, knowing Sofia's fate, those smiles haunt me.

"Sofia has a family," I state, the realization hitting me with full force. These are not just names and faces in a case file. These are real people torn apart by tragedy, their lives irrevocably altered. Niamh and I lock eyes, a silent agreement passing between us. We have to find them.

Seeing Sofia's smile and thinking of Nessa's unanswered questions, solidifies my resolve. This is more than just solving a crime; it's about bringing peace to a family shattered by loss.

"We'll find them," Niamh says, her determination mirroring my own. "For Sofia."

For a moment, the room is filled with an unspoken vow, a commitment to this cause that goes beyond curiosity or the thrill of the hunt. We're bound by a sense of justice, a need to right a wrong that's all too common in a world that often turns a blind eye to the pain of others. Sofia's story is a tragic reminder of that, but in her memory, we find our mission.

CHAPTER
TWENTY-FOUR

DIARMUID

THE WORLD OUTSIDE THE car window blurs into a palette of greens and grays as I navigate the now familiar road toward Amira's house. My attempts to reach her have been met with silence, her deliberate avoidance echoing louder than any words she might have hurled my way. It frustrates me, angers me, even. My life is busy enough as it is and chasing after Amira's dramatics is a complication I can ill afford.

Wolf knows—or at least, I think he does. That revelation alone carries the weight of a looming confrontation, a debt between us that's yet to be settled. Part of me had expected him to come at me guns blazing, quite literally, given the chance. But this version of Wolf, one that's cold, calculating, and ominously patient, is unfamiliar. It's unsettling, not knowing what to expect from him now. This isn't the man I once understood, and that unpredictability adds an edge to my already frayed nerves.

As I turn into the driveway, the extensive stretch of it reminds me of Amira's family's involvement with the Hands of the Kings. Out of the three Brides, Amira's family undoubtedly boasts the most expansive property, a fact that traces back to a time when her father, John Reardon, had ambitions aligned with those of the O'Sullivans. He was supposed to initiate the same gun trade I find myself entrenched in now. However, fate had a cruel twist in store when John, in assembling his crew, unwittingly welcomed an undercover Interpol agent into their midst.

The fallout was nearly catastrophic, threatening not just the O'Sullivans but the Hand of Kings itself. In the aftermath, Michael Reardon, the eldest son, became collateral, a hostage in a game of power and retaliation. Andrew O'Sullivan, driven by a thirst for vengeance against John, saw no solution other than death. But Victor, ever the strategist, saw potential where others saw only ruin. Thus, the Reardons were thrust into our world via a transaction of blood for loyalty, but they never received the same standing as my brothers and me.

My hand tightens on the steering wheel, the car's steady hum a contrast to the storm brewing within me.

I park in front of the house; the familiar is now a grim marker of what awaits. The front door, slightly ajar, sends a shiver down my spine. With a cautious push, I open it wider and draw my gun, the weight of it in my hand a cold comfort.

The first thing that hits me is the state of the foyer. It's a mess, a shadow of its former glory. This house, with its sprawling estate close to the shore, was designed to breathe in the fresh sea air, to stand as a testament to the Reardon's wealth and taste. Now, it's suffocating under a layer of neglect. The air is stale, thick with the scent of decay.

As I move silently through the darkened corridors, a sliver of light from the kitchen beckons. What I find there stops me in my tracks. The kitchen is in ruins. Empty bottles clutter the countertops and floor, a silent testimony to despair or madness. The sink overflows, water spilling over the broken tiles, seeping into the grout like open wounds. The destruction is complete, a cabinet door hanging off its hinges like a final, desperate cry.

With my gun leading the way, I navigate the chaos toward Amira's room. The door is off its hinges, the window wide open, curtains fluttering like ghostly sentinels. The disarray speaks of a hasty departure, or worse. "What the hell happened here?" I whisper to myself, though I'm not sure I want the answer.

A noise from the depths of the house catches my attention. I move towards it, gun ready, my heart racing. Then, he steps into the dim light—John Reardon. But he's not the man I remember. This John is a shell, his suit hanging loosely on his frame, his shirt stained and crumpled as though he's been wearing it for days.

For a moment, we just stare at each other. The standoff is surreal, a moment frozen in time amidst the wreckage of a life once lived here. This man before me, once powerful and feared, is now just another casualty of the life we've chosen. The realization doesn't bring me any comfort. If anything, it's a stark reminder of how easily everything can come crashing down.

"Where's Amira?" The demand slices through the tense air, my voice steady despite the storm raging inside me. John, looking every bit the defeated man, meets my gaze with a mix of resignation and defiance.

"I don't know," he admits, his voice barely above a whisper. "I just got home a few hours ago."

"And where have you been?"

He doesn't answer, but he doesn't have to. Rumors have a way of traveling fast in our circles, and I've heard enough to put the pieces together. "So, while you were out fucking, something happened to my Bride?" I can't keep the edge of accusation from my voice; my patience wearing thin.

He doesn't hold my eye now, and I don't know if it's his first time really looking around him, but a sense of shame washes across his face. I don't give a fuck. I want to know where Amira is.

I cock my gun for extra emphasis. "Where is Amira?"

John's hands spring up instantly. "I don't know. Amira and Tess... they don't have the best relationship," he says. He slowly drops his hands and takes another look around. "From the state I found the kitchen in, I'd say they had another row."

The implication of his words hits me like a physical blow. If there was a fight here, it wasn't just an argument; it was violent, destructive. John's lack of surprise at the violence tells its own story, a grim testament to the norm in this household.

A fury builds within me, a tidal wave of anger at the parade of shitty parents I've encountered in this world. John's mistakes have cost him dearly—Michael, taken as a hostage because of him, and two sons are dead because of his actions. And now, his only daughter is left to fend for herself against an abusive mother while he indulges in another woman. The injustice of it, the sheer negligence, pushes me over the edge.

"You leave your daughter with that woman while you're off playing Casanova?" My voice rises, a mix of disbelief and contempt. "Michael and your other sons paid for your mistakes with their lives. And now Amir a... What? She's just another casualty in your long list of failures?"

John's face crumples, the weight of my words hitting home. But my sympathy is long gone, burned away by the sight of the chaos his negligence has wrought. This isn't just about Amira or the Reardons; it's about every child left vulnerable by those who should protect them. My grip on my gun tightens, not with the intent to use it, but as a physical reminder of the control I must maintain. Losing it now won't help Amira, but every fiber of my being screams for some semblance of justice.

I want to fucking shoot him, but his dying isn't justice enough.

"She beats Amira?" I say.

He clears his throat and frowns. "You know mothers and daughters." He tries to laugh off his statement.

I put my gun away and grin at him. "No, I don't. Enlighten me."

I take a step closer to him.

"They fight."

I nod again. "She hits Amira?" I ask.

He shrugs. "She drinks a lot. Tess doesn't mean it."

My fist collides with his face, and he hits the ground hard. "Did I mean that?" I ask, kneeling over him. He's shocked for a second before he raises a shaky hand and wipes blood from his face.

I don't give him a moment to recover before I slam my fist into his face again. "Did I mean that, or did my fucking hand slip?" I roar, rage riding high with words that spill from my mouth.

My hands are around his throat, and I squeeze. I squeeze the life out of him. He deserves to die. He claws at my arms, and when his hands fall to the floor as his life slips away, I come to my senses and release him. He doesn't move or gasp for air. I stare at him for a second before he starts to gasp and rolls on his side.

He's alive.

I leave him before I finish what I started.

Fury courses through my veins. My fists clench at my sides as I stare down at him one last time, crumpled and defeated on the floor. My heart races, not with the thrill of victory, but with a ferocious concern for Amira. I need to find her, ensure she's safe from the harm that John's wife has clearly inflicted on her.

Powerful strides carry me to my car, the evening air doing little to cool the heat of my anger. My mind races as I consider where Amira might have sought refuge. The Hand of Kings manse flashes through my thoughts, but I dismiss it just as quickly. No, I had thrown her out, a decision that now twists in my gut like a knife. She wouldn't return there, not after everything.

Where could she be? The city sprawls before me, a labyrinth of possibilities and dead ends. She wouldn't be with Niamh and Selene, as they have no time for her. If it was one of them, I could go to the other for help.

Before I can start the car, my phone pierces the silence. My heart skips, hope and dread mingling in equal measure as I answer. "Do you know where your Brides are?" The voice is unfamiliar, edged with a sinister amusement that sends a shiver down my spine. Selene and Niamh are safe, accounted for, but Amira... This caller knows of her, of the danger she's in.

"I don't know who you think you are," I growl into the phone, my voice a low rumble of barely contained rage, "but you'll regret this call." My mind races, trying to place the voice.

When the caller speaks again, recognition slams into me like a physical blow. Oisin Cormick. The hitman who trained me, the man whose name I've taken as my professional moniker. Him. A flood of memories washes over me, moments of brutal training and begrudging respect. Cormick had been a constant, a harsh mentor but one who had looked out for me in his own twisted way.

All of that feels like a lie now.

"Cormick," I say, the name tasting like betrayal on my tongue. "What have you done with her?"

His laughter is cold, devoid of the warmth I once thought I knew. "Nothing. But I know where two of your Brides are, and it's somewhere they shouldn't be."

I have so many questions, like why is he tracking my Brides? He calls out an address I'm not familiar with.

I type the address into my navigation app. "I am more than twenty minutes away," I say and start up the engine.

"It's a good thing Victor gave you three." The implication of his words sends a fresh wave of urgency coursing through me. The line goes dead, and I grip the steering wheel tighter as I drive toward the address.

The man who had shaped me into the weapon I am today, who had watched over me with a cold, detached kind of care, now plays the most dangerous game with the lives of those under my protection. I have no idea why he is following my Brides, but I need to get to them. I need to protect them from Cormick and from themselves.

CHAPTER TWENTY-FIVE

NIAMH

S ofia Hughes was more than a name in a file, more than a statistic in the dark underbelly of the city. She was a person, a sister, a part of a family torn asunder by her disappearance. As I flip through the documents Rian has painstakingly gathered, I can't help but admire his diligence. For someone who's not a professional, Rian's work is impressive. The array of Sofia's social media accounts sprawls across the table, a digital footprint frozen in time. The last post dates back two years, a smiling photo that betrays no hint of the darkness to come.

This timeline doesn't add up. Sofia's death was a recent affair, yet her digital life halted long before her last breath—the discrepancy nags at me, a puzzle piece that refuses to fit.

Rian's next revelation is a stack of articles, each penned with the kind of fervor that spoke of Sofia's passion for

her work. She was a prolific writer. The majority of
names of those she interviewed were politicians. Yet,
there's a glaring gap in her professional output. No articles published in the last year of her life. What silenced
Sofia Hughes?

In the kitchen, Selene and Rian share a quiet moment
over cups of tea, the steam swirling between them. Rian
had offered me a cup, but the chaos of his apartment
made the very thought unappealing. It's not that Rian's
living conditions reflect a lack of cleanliness; rather, it's
organized chaos. Everything has its place, though that
place makes sense only to him. Selene doesn't seem to
mind the mess around us as they speak with ease over
their cup of tea.

I can't share their ease. The disorder clashes violently
with the world I grew up in, a world of precision and
predictability. My comfort zone is a rigid structure, a
framework within which I know how to operate.

But it's not the time to dwell on personal discomforts.
Sofia's life, her legacy, demands more than that. As I
sift through the documents, a plan begins to crystallize.
We need to follow the threads Sofia left behind, to trace
her last days through the shadows she chased. Her sister
deserves answers.

"Rian, how did you come across this?" I ask, motioning towards the stack of articles. My voice cuts through the comfortable silence, a reminder of the work yet undone.

Rian turns toward me. "It wasn't easy. Sofia was meticulous, maybe too much so for her own good. It's like she knew she was onto something big."

Something big. The words hang between us, heavy with implication. Sofia Hughes didn't just vanish from the digital world without reason. She was silenced, but not before she uncovered a truth someone wanted buried.

Selene's question about our next move anchors us back to the task at hand, pulling my attention momentarily away from the chaotic spread of Rian's apartment. Rian's enthusiasm is palpable as he outlines a strategy that includes reaching out to Sofia's sister, contacting secretaries of politicians entangled in Sofia's articles, and possibly even approaching the publications that had purchased her work.

As Rian speaks, my gaze drifts, taking in the layers of his obsession that wallpaper the room. Amongst the clutter, a project centered on a 'Lizzie O'Neill' with a

"1925" label catches my eye. It's a web of information, a historical puzzle he's piecing together with the patience of a saint. Close by, another collection focuses on Moll McCarthy, and I marvel at Rian's capacity to dive into the past, to resurrect stories long buried.

But it's a familiar symbol that snags my attention, halting the idle wandering of my eyes—a crown cradled in the palm of a hand. I rise, drawn to the wall, where this symbol acts as a nexus for an elaborate network of strings that branch out to maps, photographs, and timelines. It's a conspiracy theorist's dream, connecting dots between organized crime, law enforcement, and even religious figures. There, scrawled in Rian's hand, is the name "Hand of Kings."

The sight of it sends a shiver down my spine. The Hand of Kings, a name whispered in shadows, a name that has brushed against my own life in ways I wish it hadn't. I can't resist the pull of curiosity. "Tell me about this," I urge, my voice tinged with an intensity that mirrors the fixation displayed on the wall.

Rian's excitement is a tangible thing as he turns to the wall, his eyes lighting up with the fire of obsession; he leaves his tea on the counter as he approaches me and pushes his glasses up on his nose. "The Hand of

Kings," he begins, unaware that he speaks to someone far more entwined in that world than he could imagine. "I've been tracking this cult since I was a teenager. Most people laugh, call me crazy, but there are too many connections, too many coincidences. They're real, and they have their hands in everything—crime, the law, even the church."

Listening to him, I can't help but feel a twinge of fear mixed with a profound sadness. Here is Rian, a man consumed by a truth too dangerous to pursue.

"I've seen this symbol before," I confess, my voice low, laden with a weight of knowledge I wish I didn't carry. "Your work, your theories... they're not as farfetched as you might think."

Rian's eyes meet mine, a flicker of realization, of validation, passing between us.

Rian's conviction seems to grow with every word, painting a world where hidden clues and shadowy councils pull the strings of global events from behind a veil of secrecy. His theory that there's a vault filled with the world's darkest secrets, with the entrance clue hidden on a grave in Glasnevin Cemetery, sounds like something out of an adventure novel.

"A council?" Selene interjects, skepticism threading through her voice. "There isn't one leader?"

"Not from what I've discovered," Rian responds, his eyes alight with the thrill of sharing his findings.

I find myself drawn into the conversation despite my reservations. "No, wouldn't there be one guy? A Hand to guide the Kings?" I ask, trying to fit Rian's revelations into the framework of what I know.

"The Hand does the bidding of the council. Only he knows their identities," Rian clarifies, his statement echoing through the room like a prophecy. The implication of his words, the existence of someone more powerful than Victor, hangs in the air.

A thump from the hallway outside, a sudden noise that cuts through our discussion, has us all spinning toward the noise. We all freeze, our gazes snapping toward the door as if it were the only thing anchoring us to reality. Selene's whisper slices through the silence, a sharp edge of fear in her voice. "Rian, do you have a weapon?"

Rian's response is almost comical in its naivety. "Why would I have a weapon?" He looks genuinely puzzled, as if the concept of needing physical protection in his own home is a foreign one.

Rian moves toward the door, his determination masking the uncertainty that flickers in his eyes. Selene and I can only watch as he reaches for the handle, the simple act charged with the potential to change everything.

The door swings open to reveal an older man. He introduces himself as someone who works for Diarmuid, claiming concern for Selene and me. His words are smooth, with a practiced ease that belies the tension of our unexpected encounter. Rian's confusion is evident, the name Diarmuid holding no significance for him, a stark reminder of the worlds colliding at his doorstep.

The older man's smile is enigmatic. "The ladies shouldn't be here; they do not have permission." I can sense a veiled threat wrapped in politeness. I watch Rian, trying to gauge his reaction, to see if he senses the danger that's seeped into his home with this stranger's arrival. Rian's body language, open and unconcerned, betrays his inexperience and his inability to see beneath the surface of our visitor's calm demeanor.

Despite the man's unassuming appearance, something about him sets my instincts on edge. His hair, more gray than black, speaks of years and experiences far beyond what any of us can claim. And there, hidden beneath the benign exterior, is the subtle suggestion of a body honed by training.

"Who is Diarmuid?" Rian asks.

I exchange a glance with Selene, a silent communication that speaks volumes.

When Rian glances back at me, I can't find any words. He turns back to the old man. "I think it's best you leave." I don't know what Rian sees on mine and Selene's faces—fear, maybe. Dread. But he pushes the door closed.

A foot wedged in the door stops Rian from closing it. The older man pushes it open with ease and strength. When he reaches for Rian, I rush toward him, but it's a blur of movement. One minute Rian is standing there, the next the old man's arms are around his neck. Rian's death is swift, a chilling demonstration of the older man's lethal skill. The crack of his neck sends my stomach swirling. My heart beats rapidly in my ears. Blood rushes through my body at what just happened in front of us.

He killed Rian.

With a swift movement, he's in the apartment with the door closed behind him and Rian hanging lifeless from his arm. He removes a gun, and Selene screams at the same time as I jump back.

"Be quiet," he warns.

Tears run down my face, and with a shaky hand, I reach up and touch my face. I wasn't even aware that I had started crying.

"Now, get rid of all of this," he orders, his weapon sweeping the room, encompassing the entirety of Rian's life's work in one dismissive gesture.

Selene has her hands raised and nods, backing toward the wall with all its maps and connections.

I swallow bile. I can't look away from Rian's lifeless body.

"Move," I'm ordered, and I find myself with trembling hands reaching out to remove Rian's work. I can't see from the blur of tears.

As we tear it all down, he orders us to place it all in the sink. The man lowers Rian to the ground but still holds the gun toward me and Selene. The flames consume every piece of paper, every note and article, as he lights it all on fire.

Death reduces Rian's body, that was once vibrant with life and curiosity, to an object to be concealed, rolled in a rug as if he were nothing more than refuse.

Guided by the barrel of the man's gun, we move in a daze.

He swings the rug across his shoulder and opens the apartment door. "Outside." He orders.

A strangled cry falls from my lips. A hand takes mine, and I jump for a second until I look into Selene's tear-filled eyes.

The streets are silent witnesses to our grim procession. The alley was a makeshift route to an ending none of us could have predicted. The trunk of the man's car becomes Rian's final resting place, a thought that churns my stomach with a mix of rage and despair.

The man levels his gun once more. "Get in the car." His words are a sentence, mostly a death sentence.

Selene tightens her hand on mine.

"No," she says, keeping me rooted at her side.

I tremble at the cock of the gun. How can this be our end? I glance around the darkened alleyway. Something moves in the shadows. And then Diarmuid is there, a gun in his hand.

It takes me a moment to really allow what I am seeing to sink in. He has blood on his shirt, and he looks like he's been in a battle. In his eyes, there burns a fierce resolve.

The old man turns to Diarmuid. "You got here quicker than I thought." His gun is now pointed at Diarmuid.

"I was only ten minutes away. I lied," Diarmuid confesses and takes a step closer. "You will let them go, Cormick."

Cormick's smile is a flash in the darkness. "And why would I do that?"

There is a shift in the air as Diarmuid puts his gun away and steps even closer to Cormick. "You don't need a gun."

Cormick laughs. "It's a quicker way."

"If you fire that gun, people will hear." Diarmuid holds up his hands and takes another step closer to Cormick; he hasn't looked at Selene and me who are holding hands.

I want to tell Diarmuid that he killed Rian, but it's like there is no air in the alleyway.

Cormick lowers his gun, his smile no longer visible. "You want to dance? Let's dance." He whips out a knife, and my stomach sinks to my feet.

With a growl, Diarmuid moves with precision, a knife in his own hand I hadn't even seen him extract. His movements are both horrific and mesmerizing. He swipes a large arch, and the knife nicks Cormick's arm. Selene drags me back until our backs hit the wall.

Cormick retaliates instantly, his own knife drawing blood across Diarmuid's chest. I scream when I see the injury, but Diarmuid's onslaught is relentless, driven by a primal need to protect, to avenge. He swipes quickly at Cormick again, this time cutting the man's torso.

I'm waiting for his guts to spill out across the asphalt, but crimson red soaks his shirt. He hasn't a moment to recover when Diarmuid swipes out and takes his legs out from under him with one quick movement.

When Cormick hits the ground, Diarmuid is on top of him, one knee crushing the man's hand that held the knife. With a pressure that has Cormick releasing his knife, the clang of the weapon echoes. But relief that Diarmuid has the upper hand has me stepping away from the wall, thinking it's over.

"I trained you well," Cormick says before spitting to his left. Diarmuid's fist slams into Cormick's face with a viciousness that takes the remaining air from my lungs. He raises the knife and pierces one of Cormick's eyes. The sound is too much, and I want Diarmuid to stop.

"Please stop." It's all too much.

I don't think Diarmuid can hear me as he removes his knife with an eyeball hanging on the end.

"Never touch what is mine," Diarmuid says before he drives the knife deeper until only the handle sticks out of Cormic's eye, and his body goes still.

I pivot just in time as bile claws its way up my throat, and I empty the meager contents of my stomach along the alleyway wall.

Arms circle me, and I expect Selene, but it's Diarmuid. "It's okay. You are safe." He pulls me into his chest, blood soaking into my clothes, and I can't stop the sobs that take over.

"Are you hurt?" I find myself saying.

He brushes it off. "We need to leave." He doesn't look like he could walk two feet without collapsing, but he pulls me and Selene away from the gruesome scene.

"Rian, he killed Rian," I say. "We need to get him out of the trunk."

"No," Diarmuid orders as he drags us away from the bodies.

"We can't just leave him here," I object.

"It's just the way with our world," he states, a harsh truth spoken with a finality. His refusal is not cruel but a necessity born from years within a world that devours its weak and sentimental.

We leave the alleyway and Rian behind.

CHAPTER TWENTY-SIX

AMIRA

I 'VE NEVER KNOWN EMPTINESS like this. It's a void, an abyss that swallows every thought, every feeling, leaving behind a shell of who I used to be. My brothers, Dominic and Kevin, were my world, and now they're gone. Dominic's death hit like a storm, sudden and devastating. He had been the rock, the one who took on all of the responsibility after Michael was taken away. The pressure to keep our family afloat led him down paths he shouldn't have taken, risks that cost him everything. Then, there was Kevin. Watching him spiral into the abyss of drugs, trying to escape a reality too harsh to bear, was a slow torture. I knew, deep down, that it was only a matter of time for him.

Rain droplets begin to pummel the canvas above me. This is not my first night in Dublin's tent cities, and it won't be my last. But moving is life and staying in one place too long is dangerous. The thought of taking a plane out of the country is laughable—I don't even have a passport, and my finances are a joke. Sneaking onto one of the ferries has crossed my mind, but the risk of getting caught without knowing how long I'll need to stretch my meager funds is too great. This tent, my makeshift home, was a find, a bargain from a secondhand store that's become my biggest purchase in weeks.

I zip down the front of the tent and quickly zip it back up as raindrops try to enter as if they can find warmth inside my tent. They won't. It's freezing, and the angry gray sky doesn't look like it's going to give up pouring any time soon.

Hostels might have been an option, a chance for a warm bed and a shower, but they'd want identification, something I cannot give. The last thing I need is for anyone to know where I am. The fear of being found, of being dragged back into a life that's already taken everything from me, is a constant shadow.

As these thoughts swirl through my mind, I find myself mechanically opening a can of premade pasta and sauce. I don't even bother to heat it; realistically I have no way to do so.

Between mouthfuls, I shove my hands deep into the pockets of my worn jacket, seeking solace in the fleeting warmth. The cold has a way of creeping into your bones here, uninvited and relentless. Occasionally, I pause to take a sip from my water bottle. How anyone survives here in Tent City is a mystery. Two nights I've been here, and already I can sense death tapping away along with the rain on the tent.

The rain outside intensifies, its rhythm a constant backdrop to my rummaging through the clothes I picked up from the secondhand store. I'm searching for anything else I can layer. . My fingers brush against a slightly thicker sweater, and a small, triumphant smile crosses my lips. It's a minor victory in the grand scheme of things, but it's mine.

But as I layer the sweater on, the weight of my situation presses down on me with renewed vigor. Winter is approaching, and if I don't figure out what to do, it won't be the lack of a home or the constant running that will kill me—it'll be the cold. The thought sends a shiver down my spine that has nothing to do with the temperature.

As the rain ceases, I finish my pasta and sit in the tent, knowing staying here will kill me. I need to walk around and get some warmth back into my body. I'm wary, all too aware of the little I possess and how easily it could be lost or stolen. I take what's left of my money, hiding it in various parts of my clothing, securing it against my body. It's not much, but it's all I have.

Stepping out of the tent, the cold hits me anew, as if the very air sharpens its teeth against my skin. My breath forms a mist before me, a ghostly apparition in the early morning light. I pull my jacket tighter around me, huddling against the biting wind as I navigate through the camp. Around me, life stirs in muted tones, and a few faces lift in greeting, but I can't afford the luxury of acknowledgment. I can't let myself become familiar, become a part of something. The more I blend into the shadows, the safer I am.

Because of the cult that's probably still searching for my mother and me, I don't know where safety lies anymore.

As I make my way through the camp, a sudden commotion breaks out around me. People are scrambling, fear etched into their movements as they grab their belongings and flee. Through the sparse trees, the unmistakable shape of a gardai car becomes visible.

"Oh, God," I whisper to myself, a prayer to no one. The last thing I need is to be caught up in whatever is happening. With the Garda here, the camp will no longer be safe.

Not that it ever truly was.

The presence of Garda officers is overwhelming, their figures materializing from between the tents like specters of my worst fears come to life. Panic sets in, a wild, thrashing thing inside me as I try to find an escape route through the chaos. Screams pierce the early morning calm. My heart races, each beat a loud drum in my ears as I dodge and weave, desperate to remain unseen. But luck isn't on my side. After a frantic, brief chase, a firm hand closes around my arm, and I'm caught, the reality of my situation crashing down on me with the weight of a thousand bricks.

"Don't struggle." The deep male voice has me going still, and I look around as I'm led to a Garda car. I'm very aware that I'm the only one being arrested.

Sitting in the back of the Garda car, a mix of emotions courses through me. There's a twisted relief in the warmth of the car. The thought of going to jail brings with it the possibility of a warm meal. But the relief is fleeting, smothered by the realization that being booked could lead to my discovery. If my name makes it into the papers, they will find me.

The officer's phone call pierces the haze of my thoughts, a simple phrase that chills me to the bone. "I have her." The finality in his tone, the implication that I am known to them, sends a wave of dread crashing over me. This isn't just an arrest; it's a capture. They know who I am, and this changes everything. He starts the car, and I want to argue, but I already know that there is no getting away from this.

The car pulls up to a building that strikes a familiar chord of fear within me—Wolf's building. The realization hits me like a physical blow. Diarmuid has rejected me, discarded me to the whims of fate without so much as a backward glance. I am to be passed straight to the bottom, no bargaining, no chance of mercy. The officer's demeanor is icy, his eyes never meeting mine, as if I'm already condemned, already nothing.

This is it—the end of the line. All my running, all my hiding, has led to this moment—the fear, the cold, the loneliness. Diarmuid's rejection is a sentence worse than any jail could impose, a fate I'd been desperate to avoid.

As I'm led into the building, each step feels heavier than the last. The warmth of the car is a distant memory, replaced by the cold reality of my situation. I'm entering the lion's den, a place where mercy is a foreign concept and survival is a game played by rules I no longer understand.

The sensation of not having to fight anymore washes over me with an almost surreal relief. For so long, I've been running, dodging, hiding—survival was my only goal. Now, as I'm led into the lobby by the officer, the fight seems to drain out of me, leaving behind a weary acceptance of whatever fate awaits.

Wolf is there.

"Thank you, officer," he says with a fresh smile.

The officer releases me and nods at Wolf. His departure is swift, leaving me alone with Wolf, the architect of my current predicament. He gestures for me to follow, and I do, my body moving of its own accord, my mind numb to the implications of his command.

As we walk, a heavy dread settles in my stomach, a weight so profound it threatens to drag me down. I can imagine the horrors that might await me, each scenario more terrifying than the last. A voice in the back of my mind whispers that death might be preferable to what lies ahead.

Wolf's voice cuts through my dark reverie. "I have a present for you." The word sends a chill through me. As we approach a door, the sound of screaming filters through, a warning of the nightmare to come. He opens the door, and the scene that unfolds is something out of a twisted fantasy.

My mother, the woman who gave me life, is tied to a post in the center of the room, a spectacle of despair. Her eyes are wild, filled with an animalistic fear as she screams and twists, more monster than human. The room is lined with tables that hold an array of implements: weapons, syringes, bottles, blindfolds, and even a stereo. It's a tableau of torture, a display of human depravity.

"I went to your home to find you, but I found your mother instead." Perverse satisfaction laces Wolf's voice.

Like a circus presenter, he holds out his arms towards my mother. "A present for you."

The sight of her, so broken and lost, ignites something within me—a rage, a sorrow, a desperate urge to protect, even now.

As my mother's gaze locks onto mine, the air shifts. The pitiable creature I saw moments ago vanishes, replaced by the all-too-familiar specter of anger and venom that I grew up with. Her curses fill the room, each word a barb that finds its mark with practiced ease. The years of verbal abuse, the emotional scars—they all come flooding back as she lunges at me, restrained only by her bonds.

In a moment of raw, unfiltered emotion, I clutch my jaw, stepping into the room with a determination I hadn't known I possessed. My eyes fixate on one of the tables, and without thinking, I grab a bat. My grip is tight, knuckles white as I advance, every step fueled by years of suppressed anger and hurt. But before I can swing, my arm is caught in an iron grasp. Wolf's smile is chilling, a silent reminder of the power he holds in this moment.

"When was the first time she hurt you?" he asks, his voice calm.

The memory surfaces unbidden—Dominic's funeral, six years ago, a day when grief was met with cruelty instead of comfort.

"Six years ago. At Dominic's funeral." I say, still looking at my mother. She's still struggling, still screaming at me, telling me I'm a whore. I'm useless.

"If you hurt her now, it will be over in a moment. A lifetime of hurt deserves a lifetime of pain." He releases my arm as if allowing me to make my choice.

He steps behind me and speaks in my left ear.

"LSD is coursing through her veins. You could create nightmares for her." He steps to my left.

"You could be the architect of her terror." He smiles at me.

"Why? Why do this for me?" I ask a question that feels too small for the gravity of this moment.

He exhales and glances at my mother, who's still struggling. "I feel a kinship with you. The world hasn't been kind to either of us."

The revelation is unsettling. To be seen, understood, and aided by someone like Wolf—a man capable of such cruelty yet ready to offer solace in revenge—is to stand at the edge of an abyss. The choice before me is stark: to embrace the darkness offered as salvation or to reject it.

I have no one else. No one who sees me like Wolf does. Diarmuid has cast me aside, and in the space of a moment, I make my mind up.

I hand the bat to Wolf. "The world has been fucking cruel," I snarl and he smiles.

CHAPTER
TWENTY-SEVEN
SELENE

T HE INTERIOR OF DIARMUID'S townhouse is bathed in the soft glow of evening light. But tonight, the elegance of my surroundings is marred by the scene unfolding within its walls. Diarmuid stands at the center, a figure of defiance and pain, his shirt clinging to his skin with blood. Cuts and bruises litter his skin, and one of his knuckles looks to be broken.

I can't think about what happened to Rian. I can't think about the violence that I watched pour from Diarmuid. A man always so finely dressed, well presented...I never would have known such darkness lived inside him. But he protected me and Niamh.

"Sit down," I say to him, He looks ready to fall down. He does, slumping into a white plush couch. Niamh has already gone to the kitchen, and I hear water running. I think her mind is as fumbled as mine.

I stand over Diarmuid, trying to figure out where to start. When Niamh returns with water and a washcloth, we work in tandem. She hands me one, and I start to mop up some of the blood on Diarmuid's arm, each stroke showing me the blood isn't his. He had arrived with blood on him…who else had he killed?

Diarmuid pushes our hands away. His phone is in his hand, and he keeps hitting a call button. The noise of the engaged tone has his worry growing.

"Have you seen Amira?" he asks.

I glance at Niamh and shake my head.

"No," Niamh says.

He hits the call button again. I had always thought Amira to be overdramatic, her tendency to find trouble a constant source of irritation. But tonight, the fear in Diarmuid's eyes mirrors my own. Despite everything, despite the harsh words and harsher feelings between Amira and myself, the thought of her in danger, potentially facing death, is a cold wake-up call. She may be a bitch, but she doesn't deserve to die.

I start to open the buttons of his shirt, and he continues to call Amira. Each time I hear the dead line, my stomach drops a little further again. There is so much blood on his chest, and this time it's his own. The largest cut was from Cormick.

"You need stitches," I say as I hold the cloth to his chest.

"I was supposed to keep you all safe, protect you from harm." His voice rises. He doesn't seem to be aware of the damage that was inflicted on him. Niamh washes his free hand, and he hisses as she rubs across his damaged knuckles.

"Sorry." Her voice is a whisper.

Diarmuid seems to come out of the fog he is under and looks at Niamh. "I'm sorry," he says, the gentleness in his voice bringing tears to Niamh's eyes.

"My sister, Ella. I need to get her. She could be in danger."

Diarmuid nods. "I will find her and protect her."

Niamh sniffles. "Thank you."

"I will take the four of you somewhere safe." His hopes for Amira are still high.

When Diarmuid looks at me, fire lights up in his eyes.

"Why were you at Rian's apartment?" I can hear the jealousy in his voice.

The intensity of his gaze is unnerving.

"We heard there was a body placed on top of Andrew O'Sullivan's, and we wanted to know who she was."

He's glaring at me. His reaction is a mixture of concern and barely contained fury.

"How could you be so stupid?" His voice is grave, and I'm stunned at the level of venom in his words.

"I needed to know more about you. I needed to learn about what I might be marrying into." My words send my heart racing. I did this to learn about him.

"Jesus, Selene. This ends now. Do you understand how dangerous this is? Someone wants that murder covered up, and they will stop at nothing."

I nod because the moment I watched Rian die, I knew we had gone too far.

"How do you not want to know who killed your uncle?" Niamh asks. I know her mind is still on Ella. If Ella had died in such a brutal way, she would want to know who killed her.

"I already know who killed Andrew O Sullivan," Diarmuid says. Something shifts in his gaze, and he glances from me to Niamh. "I did."

His confession seems to draw the very air from the room. The murder of Andrew O'Sullivan wasn't just another headline in the news; it was a deed done by Diarmuid's own hand.

I want to ask why, but I can't bring the words to my lips.

Niamh quietly excuses herself, retreating to the sanctuary of the guest bedroom. Her departure is a silent echo of the turmoil that Diarmuid's confession has stirred within us.

At Diarmuid's words, I dropped the washcloth, and blood found its way onto the white sofa. I watch it soak in.

"I'm going for a shower." Diarmuid rises, and I give him some space as I try to process what he just told us. He killed Andrew O'Sullivan.

He killed Cormick, too, to save us. Maybe he had his reasons for killing Andrew. My stomach continues to curl, and I find myself following him. I never thanked him for saving us. Our fate would have been in the hands of Cormick, and most likely, right now, we would be rotting in a shallow grave.

I open the door to thank him, my words poised on the tip of my tongue, but they die away at the sight that greets me. Reflected in the mirror, Diarmuid's back is a tapestry of scars, each mark a story of pain endured, of survival against odds that would break lesser men. The scars, numerous and brutal, speak of hundreds of strokes of the whip, each one a testament to his torment.

My heart clenches at the sight, a mix of horror, sorrow, and an indescribable urge to reach out, to somehow ease the pain that each scar represents. "What happened to you?" The question is out before I can think, a demand for understanding, for the story behind the scars that mar the skin of a man who has become an enigma. Did Andrew do this? Is that why he killed him? But these marks are years in the making.

Diarmuid's shoulders tense, and he turns to me. His chest is marred with fresh cuts. Jesus, he has endured so much.

"Andrew and Victor had a very unique way of punishing me." His words bring tears to my eyes. No one should suffer like this.

"That's why you killed him?" I ask and swallow the sorrow that threatens to consume me.

"I will kill Victor, too." His words should terrify me, should have me running from him.

"Good," I say as tears make a pathway down my cheeks.

The man before me is not just a protector. He is a survivor, carrying the weight of his past with every step, every decision marked by the trials he has endured. The revelation does not weaken my perception of him; rather, it deepens my respect and my understanding of the battles he has fought, those both visible and those hidden beneath the surface.

"Rian spoke of a council, one that's even higher than Victor."

"I know it's deeper than they allow me to see. But I will find every player."

I step deeper into the bathroom. "I'll help you."

He immediately shakes his head. "I won't let you get hurt."

"I won't give up." I raise my head. Seeing the marks on his body has solidified my decision.

Diarmuid steps closer to me and takes my face in his hands. "Troublemaker," he says with a soft smile.

"But we must find out what happened to Sofia Hughes. I can't let it go, Diarmuid," I state.

He rests his forehead against mine. "Okay, Troublemaker."

I lean back so I can look up at him. "Now, get in the shower." He needs to wash off the blood; we need to see the true extent of his injuries.

He slowly takes off his trousers, his back to me again, and my heart squeezes. I want to ask when the abuse started, but instead, I peel off my clothes. He glances at me for a brief moment but finishes getting undressed. The water pours from the showerhead, and he steps in under the spray. I grab a washcloth and enter the shower with him.

He's facing me, and all of a sudden, I'm nervous and heartbroken, but I swallow the emotions and start to wash him down.

He hisses now and then but closes his eyes. "I have sent men to find Amira and bring Ella here."

I nod but remember he can't see me. "Okay," I say.

He glances down at me, and his large hand covers mine. He loosens the cloth from between my fingers and starts washing me. I allow it. I need some form of kindness now after all the violence. My parents never showed me any affection, and I lean into this moment with Diarmuid. My hands rise up, and I touch his broad shoulders, allowing them to run down his arms. This is why he never took his shirt off. He was hiding the brutality that was inflicted on him.

The water pours down his chest, the stream of blood turning from red to pink. He still needs stitches, but the cut isn't as ugly as I thought it would be.

"Cormick trained you?" I ask as my hands trail down to his elbow before running along his forearms.

"Yes, as an assassin."

My heart races, and I look into his steel eyes. I need to know.

"Did you kill a child?" I ask.

He tilts his head, the cloth he was using to wash me forgotten.

"No."

I can't help the relief that floods my body. "Was each death for the greater good?" I ask.

This time, his gaze shadows over. "No," he answers honestly.

I nod.

"I just do as I'm instructed." He sounds so tired.

He tilts my chin up so I'm looking at him. "But, I won't for much longer. I'll take you all somewhere safe."

I want to ask him how he really thinks that will play out, but time will tell.

His lips brush mine, and they are warm and gentle as he kisses me, like he's sealing our fates deeper together.

Stepping into the shower with Diarmuid was a choice. My one move in this game of kings and pawns...perhaps the only one worth making.

But mine, nonetheless.

My choice right now is to kiss him back, our mouths moving together assuredly with passion and conviction. I am no longer a pawn in this game.

I'm now a player.

CHAPTER TWENTY-EIGHT

AMIRA

As Wolf leads me down to the basement, my heart races. I wonder if my mother is still alive or has the constant pumping of drugs into her system taken her away. The stairway creaks under our weight, each step sending a shiver through me. At the bottom, a single bulb casts long shadows on the walls.

I spot my mother huddled in the corner of the cage. Her hands cover her head, and her knees are buried in her face. Does she look thinner? I'm not sure. Wolf's fingers graze mine, and I glance up at him.

"I want to show you something." A slow smile creeps along her lips as he guides me to a small, cold room at the far end. There, I see her—the maid who had struck me, now confined within a rusty iron cage. My stomach churns at the sight, a mix of fear and vindication swirling inside me. Her wrists are covered in white bandages, her hands gone. Diarmuid really had them cut off.

The idea sends butterflies bursting through my belly.

The maid is standing with her back to me, her handless arms hanging at her sides.

Wolf pulls a chair close to the cage and motions for me to sit. As I do, he perches on an old crate across from me, his eyes never leaving my face. "Amira, I want to tell you a story," he begins, his voice steady but filled with intensity.

He reaches into his pocket and takes out a small gold box. He opens it, and inside, I see white powder.

I know what this is: cocaine. After slicing the cocaine into fine, thin lines, he uses a note and rolls it tight. With one end at his nostril and the other at the start of the line, he inhales the powder before standing and walking toward me. "I think it's best you have some before I tell you the story."

I take the note and repeat what he just did. The rush is immediate and Wolf laughs when I sneeze and scrunch up my nose.

"First time?" he asks. The gold box disappears back into his pocket, and he sits back on the crate.

I blink several times. Everything seems more focused, more defined. The maid still has her back to me in a show of pure disrespect.

"Amira!" My voice reaches my ear in a sing-song note. I turn to Wolf, who grins. "I want to tell you a story." I sit up. "Tell me."

"There once was a princess who was loved deeply by her three brothers, surrounded by warmth and affection. But tragedy struck, and two brothers died, leaving her vulnerable."

I snort. I wasn't a princess, but when Wolf narrows his eyes at me, I keep my sarcasm to myself.

"Her mother, consumed by grief and madness, turned against her, the once kind touches now twisted into pain. The princess was eventually handed off to a man named Diarmuid, who promised protection but soon abandoned her as well."

That part has me shifting in my seat. He had dumped me outside without a second glance. Left me to fend for myself on the street with no one. I bet he hasn't even looked for me.

"And then," Wolf's voice grows softer, "a prince came. He offered her a life where she'd never be alone again, a life where she could exact revenge on those who wronged her."

My hands tremble in my lap as he speaks, the story weaving into the fabric of my own life, mirroring the abandonment and pain I've known.

He reaches under his seat and produces an axe, the metal glinting ominously in the dim light. He offers it to me with a solemn nod. "I will give you a world of cages that will hold your enemies, Amira. A world where you can be the queen of your own justice."

As I take the axe, feeling its weight in my hands, a dark satisfaction fills me. Images of Niamh and Selene, the sources of so much of my misery, locked away as this maid is now, dance through my mind. I can't help but smile—a cold, hard smile that doesn't quite reach my eyes.

"Now, let them know they have messed with the wrong person," Wolf says, his voice a low growl as he strides to the cage and swings the door open. The maid's screams pierce the silence, her terror a stark contrast to the calm that settles over me.

With the axe in hand, I stand, my resolve hardening. Today marks the end of my victimhood and the beginning of something new—something fierce. As Wolf steps back, watching me with an approving gaze, I know I've crossed into a realm from which there is no return. My heart, once fragile, now beats a violent rhythm, ready to claim what is mine by right of pain and survival.

FIND OUT WHAT HAPPENS NEXT IN "WHEN KINGS BEND."

About the author

When Vi Carter isn't writing dark romance books, you can find her reading her favorite authors, baking, taking photos, or watching Netflix.

Married with three children, Vi divides her time between motherhood and all the other hats she wears as an Author.

Social Media Links for Vi Carter

Store: https://author-vicarter.com/

Facebook Reader Group: Carters Crew

Made in United States
North Haven, CT
18 June 2024

53780947R00183